End

Also by Barbara Adair
In Tangier We Killed the Blue Parrot

End

Barbara Adair

First published by Jacana Media (Pty) Ltd in 2007

10 Orange Street
Sunnyside
Auckland Park 2092
South Africa
+2711 628 3200
www.jacana.co.za

© Barbara Adair, 2007

All rights reserved.

ISBN   978-1-77009-305-8

Cover design by miss sweden
Set in Sabon 11/14pt
Printed by CTP Book Printers, Cape Town
Job No. 000503

See a complete list of Jacana titles at www.jacana.co.za

*One might have said that this man
passed through life without leaving any trace...
and one might even claim that he had no victims.*

Soren Kierkegaard, *The Seducer's Diary*

Prologue

With the coming of the wars, many eyes in imprisoned Africa turned hopefully, or desperately, towards the freedom of America, the freedom to live and the freedom not to die. Johannesburg became the great embarkation point, but not everybody could get to Johannesburg directly, and so, a torturous roundabout refugee trail sprang up. A route of wild thoughts and ill-timed fabrications, through Maputo, Beira, across the Zambezi River. Some travelled by train, others on foot, but only the fortunate ones, through money or influence or maybe just luck, make it out of the abyss and scurry on to Johannesburg, and from Johannesburg to America. And the others wait... and wait... and wait... and wait.

I

Can Freddie tell you a story, a fiction; words that mean nothing or everything depending upon how you want to perceive them? And will it have a wow finish? 'Hey Mister, I met a man once when I was a kid.'

The last time he saw X was in the Caminhos de Ferro City Railway Station, the train station in Maputo. Around them people ran back and forth. A hectic fevered excitement seemed to have overcome all of those who wanted to get out of the city. He remembered that they said goodbye under the large clock that was on Platform 15. Platform 15 was the only platform that was working in the station and the trains snaked along it, creeping and crawling. The other platforms just consisted of tracks, lonely untrained tracks. He thought for a minute, what did it remind him of? Then Freddie reminded him, she whispered in his ear, '*Casablanca*; that scene when Rick is waiting for Ilsa at the station in Paris.'

Ah yes, he remembered it now. It is pouring with rain, the black and white raindrops bouncing off Rick's grey fedora and onto his face. He stands under the clock on the platform, looking constantly at his watch and waiting for her. A lone man amidst a crowd of people. He reaches his hand up and touches his head. His hair is dry.

It was not raining in Maputo. And he did not wear a hat. 'This reminds me of that scene in the movie *Casablanca*,' he said to X.

'What scene?' X asked. 'I remember seeing it, but it was so long ago.'

'It's that scene on the station platform in Paris. It's raining and Rick is waiting for Ilsa. They are leaving Paris to escape the Nazis, but she does not arrive...'

'I've had a lovely time these last few days,' X interrupted him. 'I can't stay with you now... don't ask me why. I wish I could. Go now, my sweet darling boy. Remember to send me the photographs... you used black and white film didn't you? They should be good.' As he held X's hand he said the name to himself, X. X can't even understand this, he thought, this clock on the platform, and the fact that we are standing below it to say goodbye.

Freddie looked at him, jealously, watching as if through the slats of a window. He was so far away. 'Can I hold your hand now?' she said to him. But he did not reply, he just sighed and held X's hand more tightly. He felt that if he let the hand go he would never hold it again, and he did not want to let it go. If he let go the hand it would be gone forever. The image of Rick was still in his mind.

'Thanks Freddie, for reminding me of the movie,' he said. 'It has made things so much more complicated; now I will have to think about love and romance... love and loss.'

'No you won't,' Freddie replied. 'I'll have to deal with the clichés. After all, I'm the writer, the author. I'm writing this story. I'm the genuine creator. And if Martin Amis can do it in *London Fields*, well I can too. Wait for me. I'll walk down streets I've never been to. I'll meet characters I know I'll never know. I might even fly away.' Freddie turned to him. 'Do you think this is an unoriginal style?' But she didn't wait for him to reply. 'Is there anything that is original? Some writers just do unoriginality better than others.'

It was Maputo, not Paris, so it was not raining. The waning sun shone down margarine yellow. It clung wet garment-like on the walls of the monolithic station and draped itself over the arching roof. It was hot even though the sun was already setting. The station was outdated now; European architecture with Art Deco mosaics decorating the walls, a peppermint green design that was going slightly mouldy. Everything in Maputo had that slightly aged look. The ever-present Portuguese, now old and dying, had, as something new, adolescent, tried to become adult. The death of the Portuguese in Africa. The building reminded him of the fascist architecture in Europe, the station in Milan, Mussolini's last stand, Mussolini's mausoleum. Everything reeked of death in the station that night; his breath like the dying embers of a fire, the scrawny chicken that was going home for supper, the robust ticket seller who demanded 100 Meticais over and above the ticket price for a seat in first class. And first class was empty anyway. Death and darkness. He knew it would be dark when he eventually left the station, dark and hot. The sultry tropical air would embrace him, much like X had embraced him in those white sheets. Those white shrouds.

'It must have been passionate for you to come up with this death and dying description,' Freddie said to him as she felt the feel of the city and read the words. 'But you're not the first to think of death and sex together, sex and murder... The Marquis de Sade...' But who was passionate, he or she, or maybe just the Marquis?

He continued to speculate without thinking of Freddie. Strange how they said goodbye under that clock. Rick was leaving Paris to the Nazis and he left alone. He was leaving X in a beautiful fascist building, and X was returning to London. And he would leave alone. He kissed X on the mouth. For a moment he thought that he just might love X if he got the chance. Would Freddie give him the chance, he wondered. Michael Curtis gave Rick and Ilsa that chance and what happened? They were immortalised in black and white close-up shots. Maybe he would get a chance this time, maybe this time.

'You're already immortal. Words don't die. They just have to be read. It's only the readers that die,' Freddie said to him. Simultaneously Freddie thought, Fuck, now I have the archetypal lone hero on my hands who doesn't want to be the lone hero. What other lone heroes can I use as a model to describe him? Did they all want to be heroes? Did they want to be heroes at all? Or do all of us, the reading public, make ordinary people doing ordinary things into heroes – commodities? She thought for a minute. Oh well, what does it matter? Che's bloodied and tortured body lying on the Bolivian planks in the barracks, alone in a postcard. Rick, where I'm going you can't follow. What I've got to do you can't be any part of. I'm no good at being noble, but... which ones didn't fulfil the cliché, or did they all fulfil it?

A whistle blew. 'It's the last call, X. The train will soon leave,' he said. X climbed aboard the train. He handed him what was left of a burnt out cigarette. He thought he heard X say, 'Here's looking at you, Kid,' but he must have been mistaken, for X had never looked at him, looked into him.

And, Freddie reminded him, 'X doesn't even know that he's in a movie, so how would he know what words to say?'

And then X was gone, up and into the train. He turned and walked along the platform. He put the burning ember between his lips, his full lips. His mouth drank in the smoky air. The coal glowed, but only for a moment. Then the smoke curled above his head. It filled him. He crushed the butt out on the sole of his shoe and threw it into a nearby dustbin. He never did look back to see if X waved to him from the open window of the carriage. Rick never looked back, so why should he? And when Freddie looked back she saw that X did not wave from the open window.

As he walked back down the Avenida Patrice Lumumba he felt the tears from behind his eyelids drip down his cheeks. He turned to look in a shop window and his reflection looked back out at him. For a moment he thought he saw a mark, a scar on his forehead, a bullet wound. But then as he moved he saw that it was only a shadow cast by a curved and bent lamppost. There was no wound after all. Only a few tears, and those he knew would soon be gone, dried by the slight breeze that blew up from the sea. Forgotten as he went about his life. Forgotten like the people after whom the streets were named, a city of dead and dying heroes. The dirt of his grave was already sprinkled on his face.

He wondered if he really should be thinking of X as he walked down this street. How inconsequential their little interlude must seem in the vast space of history. As he walked he wondered if he truly was the deep thinking philosophical type, and if so, if he would really be thinking in these images, in this way? Sex was on his mind. But then, he rationalised to himself, maybe it was Freddie who had sex on her mind, not him.

And then, as if she could read his mind – well, she could read his mind – she interrupted his inner reverie. 'Yes,' she said, 'you must think these images. Readers like a man with personal integrity, morality, intelligence. They want to be able to identify with the hero, they want an identity, they want to be saved from the obscurity of having a choice. You can't just think about love or sex, whatever it is. Think about the man after whom this street is named – Patrice Lumumba. His violent death, his desperate escape across the Congo to Stanleyville, the jubilant celebratory bonfires along the way, which made it so much easier for his pursuers to follow him, his final revolting martyrdom. Did you know that the big tree under which he died is still full of bullets?' But he would not; he refused to think about these things. All he could think about was the smell of dried semen on his fingers, on his lips, its taste down his throat. It iced over his heart and reached down his thighs.

Freddie reached into her bag, a black bag that contained everything anyone would need for a journey. She took out a tissue and slowly wiped the tears from his face. It must be sad, this kind of leaving, she thought, especially as she knew who X was; a fraud from Johannesburg. He did not leave Johannesburg because he absconded with the church funds. He did not leave because he ran off with the senator's husband. He did not leave because he killed a man. He is not, after all, Rick. But who is Rick in this story? And then, with a confused frown, she thought, what the hell does dried semen smell like anyway?

And as the tears continued to slide down his face, and as Freddie gently wiped them away, she realised that, even though she had created him, this unnamed protagonist, she loved him. She had wanted so badly to hold his hand on that platform – to hold him now. Instead she leant over and kissed him, not a passionate kiss, for passion is reserved only for X. X, whom he still wanted to kiss. Freddie knew, knew that only she could love him, but the lie was always in the kiss, a betrayal.

Tick, tock, tick, tock… Time is fleeting, madness takes its toll. How does the rest of the song go? And soon this story will end… Tick, tock, tick, tock… Time goes by… After time comes time…

Freddie leaned towards him as he continued to walk down the Avenida. 'Alexandre Gustave Eiffel designed the station in Maputo, the same architect who designed the Eiffel Tower,' Freddie said. 'A little bit of Paris in Africa. I think he designed something in Libreville too,' Freddie continued. 'Eiffel was exiled from French society because he was a fraud, so he designed for the second best, the third… the fourth best. He never set foot in the places where his buildings were erected; this city, Libreville. He never left Paris. The station is the home of fraud now.' She walked onwards. 'I suppose Rick will always have Paris, and you, you will always have Maputo,' Freddie said. But he did not reply. He was moody and brooding. He had just left the person he thought he was in love with, so she accepted his silence.

'Love,' Freddie mused, 'that human construct. Love for a person, love for a country, love for a cause. Unrequited love, requited love that is dull enough to make a person search for another love, hope for love, the journey to find love and glory. After all, who said it? "What is the point of war without love?" The love themes can go on and on. I wonder if there's a novel in which this theme is not present?' She turned to him. 'You can love X. I'll let you love him, just for the moment, just for now.'

End

Now they walked into a crowded street, a more popular part of the city. A policeman, who looked like a soldier, was walking ahead of them. He suddenly stopped and looked around. He looked at his watch. Freddie wondered why time was so important to him. Did he have someone to kill at an appointed hour? Then the policeman felt in his pocket and pulled out a whistle. He blew it hard. A young man with dreadlocks in his hair and wide-angled eyes began to run. He looked wildly around him, searching for a place to hide, a doorway into which he could creep. There was nowhere. The policeman, the whistle clamped between his lips, ran towards him. There was fear on the young man's face. His eyes were glowing, the eyes of an animal caught in headlights. The policeman took the whistle from his mouth and shouted out something in Portuguese. Maybe it was 'halt', maybe it was 'what are you doing here', but the young man did not stop running.

The sound of a shot. A gun is fired. The bullet pushes itself between the young boy's shoulder blades. He is propelled forward by its force. He falls to the ground and lies there motionless, his blood silently pumping from his back. It is black as it mingles with the dark water of the drain into which he has fallen. A fat rat with long whiskers runs to him and nuzzles his open mouth. Above him on the wall Samora Machel looks out across the street. His radiant smile is benign. The policeman bends down over the young man. He looks in his pockets, the pockets of the tattered trousers. He pulls out some documents. Freddie, who is now close to the dead boy, leans over to look at what the policeman holds in his hands. A few pieces of dirty paper – a few pages of Frelimo propaganda.

'Well,' said Freddie, 'I think they might have got the wrong man, or in this case, boy.'

The policeman got up. He shrugged his shoulders. He walked onwards. The crowd gathered around the dead boy. Someone rushed forward, also a young boy in tattered clothes. The whites of his eyes shone in anticipation. He pulled at the dead boy's shoes. His own feet were bare. Now they had shoes

7

to protect them. Another boy moved forward and grabbed at the bag that hands no longer grasped. A bare-breasted child, not more than ten years old, carefully took off the dead boy's striped shirt so as not to get too much blood on it. But it was bloody anyway and had a hole in the back and the front. Better than nothing. He wanted to get as little blood on it as possible. Soon the dead youth had little left except his brown, stained underwear. No one seemed to want that, and so, with a little dignity, he was left wearing something.

Freddie was silent. He said nothing. They both just walked and looked. The silence gave Freddie time to think, about him, and X, and death and history. What about society, she thought. All novels have some social element to them. Probably because people don't live near Walden Pond, they live in a social world. And so they devise some internal drama for themselves. I must devise an internal drama. But I must also justify this internal drama; give it some validity, something that makes readers think that they are not just indulging in an individual stage show. I must create a context, a public social production: genocide, racism, poverty. It's endless, Freddie thought, the way the same themes can be written about over and over again. And what did the reader really think of all this, these clichés? Were there enough of them to make the story moving, or were they simply laughable, she wondered. Well, she didn't really care; after all, she would only be here for the length of this novel. Once it ended, she and this created world would no longer exist. Only the readers would continue to exist in their own worlds, worlds that they created in which to pass their own time.

II

Sitting down to write the next chapter, Freddie remembered that she had once read a magazine piece that described an exhibition of body parts. She could not remember where the exhibition was, or where she had seen the article, but the description stayed in her mind. She slipped the diskette into the computer and thought to include it in this chapter, the juxtaposition of views. Maybe, she thought, the description could be in a magazine that her character finds at the airport – better still, part of an in-flight magazine. As she settled at the computer, her coffee next to her, Freddie wondered whether the character should become a she, a trans-gendered character... So much more interesting, she thought. Yes, a she, a me, and an I.

She wondered if X should enclose the article in a letter. No, X would not do this. She knew him better than anyone else could ever know him and he did not send letters. Would her unnamed protagonist still love X if he sent a letter with a description of this exhibition? Well, no matter, X would not send the description. But she would describe it anyway, fit it into the narrative somewhere – after all, this kind of contrast is a literary device; more especially as the description of the exhibition is not in any way related to this story.

The magazine lay on the table next to the bed. It was not a magazine that she – not Freddie, but the I, the he, the she, the changeable-at-a-whim character – would normally read. In-flight magazines never really held her attention with their vacuous descriptions of good restaurants and places to visit.

They were magazines for tourists, and she was but a traveller who would never be returning home. But she had put it in her bag nonetheless and she wondered why. Maybe just because they were handing out free copies of it at the baggage check-in counter. She lay back against the rock-beige pillow and stared at the grey ceiling. She looked at the printed page in front of her. *Visit Exotic Tropical Island – two for the price of one. A Romantic Night Out in the City – just you and the one you love.* Then she read the description of an exotic, or maybe it was erotic, exhibition that had been held in Berlin, an exhibition of body parts. Freddie wondered what her expression would be after she had read the article. But when she had, she was blank, no wistful smile, no grimace, nothing.

A rather bizarre exhibition of body parts went on show at A Gallery in Berlin. The exhibition combines art and anatomy, using real bodies. The artists have treated and dissected the bodies using a technique called plastination. Although there's a strong design element, it's all dressed up as medical science. The public interest is, however, not entirely scientific. Some of the exhibits are interesting, but also disturbing. There are two women who died in childbirth, one standing and the other reclining in a maternal, faintly erotic pose... both skinned so that you can see only exposed muscle. The one woman's parts have been opened through dissection so one can see a baby in utero. Another is of a man standing with his right arm up, as if holding a coat over his shoulder and about to head off down a Milan catwalk... except that over his shoulder is his entire skin, like a leather jacket. The bodies are cut into vertical slices and there is one in which you can see a complete arterial system, the rest of the body has been removed. There are also a number of foetuses at various stages of in-utero development. The show could be interpreted as quite a strong critique of abortion as the public can see how well developed these children are after only four weeks. Many have criticised this exhibition for being unethical, although their reasoning has not been fully explored. Whatever the ethics of the exhibition, it is riveting.

She put the magazine down on the table next to the bed on which she was seated, cross-legged like Buddha, contemplating the god within her, and turned to look out of the bungalow window. The window was small, barred and dirty. The dust from the nearby airstrip was constant. It never seemed to let up. It coated everything in a warm honey brown. On some days it was so thick that when she took off her sunglasses the skin on her face that had been covered by the big black lenses was set apart from the rest of her, white circles in the middle of brown. The window of the small room was closed, for the dust and the mosquitoes supposedly, but also because she wanted to keep out the sounds of the nearby camp, which never seemed to diminish. The constant chatter in Portuguese, or other languages that she could not understand, the screams and the crying. It was the crying that got to her the most because it was never very loud, just there in the background, a quiet and constant river. Tears falling into the dust.

She had flown up the day before, from Maputo. It was a small six-seater Cessna run by *Médecins Sans Frontières*, the 'barefoot doctors', as her hack colleagues commonly called them. And although she ridiculed them as much as her colleagues did, sometimes she felt a strange sense of yearning to be one of them, these barefoot doctors and nurses. They were real people. They had a real purpose. They had all crossed borders, the border of the 'I' that Freddie had created for her. They knew that they were 'I'. They had manufactured a meaning for themselves.

'I is always another,' Freddie said, as if she had heard her thoughts.

But her thoughts would not be contained. It saddened her. The barefoot doctors would be rewarded in heaven, whereas she would not be rewarded. Freddie had given her no meaning except the emptiness of love. The doctors and nurses, they never seemed to be concerned with that trite inner turmoil that constantly plagued her. Did X really love her, or was she just someone he had met, fucked and then left behind him? Why didn't he write to her, she thought. He had promised. She felt an emotion she could not describe; it was so overwhelming a tear crept out of one of her eyes and ran down her cheek. Then it dripped off her face and fell to the dusty floor. 'I have given you an expected tear,' said Freddie, 'because I want readers to think that this inner turmoil is meaningful, but somehow incomplete. Perhaps they will compare it to what is going on outside this bungalow and think that what is happening there is so terrible, unspeakable. It is a terrible beauty, and your emotions, well they should be beautiful, but they will seem so pedestrian, banal. Is it all just a cliché?' Can I, Freddie wondered, put in so many clichés? Her fingers moved, as if to delete the paragraph. Then they stopped, hovering in the air above the keyboard. Oh well, two clichés in a story can make you laugh, a hundred clichés, she laughed, they will move you. Sometimes, Freddie thought, extreme banality allows you to catch a glimpse of the sublime, the glorious incoherence of the sublime, the glorious incoherence of the prosaic.

She felt shocked. She didn't want to cry. She wanted to be a concerned person there to help. Why was Freddie doing this to her? Instead, she just said sadly to Freddie, 'These doctors, the ones who try to stop the tears, they live human lives, just like me. And you have put me in a trap. I feel like a fly with my feet stuck in wax. I am trapped in the world that is your world.'

She got up off the bed and walked towards the door. She needed to work. The story for the newspaper was incomplete. It needed a human touch. It needed some of the tears of another, some human tears.

She bent over to pick up her notebook and suddenly felt a familiar pain in her stomach that reached from the end of her lungs right down into the top of her thighs. Her period – it must be, it was the right time. Oh, thank god, she thought, as she remembered the ecstasy she had shared with X in the king-size bed. She remembered how they had laughed, knowing that the people in the next-door room could hear their passion. She remembered that they hadn't used a condom. She, because how could she care about dying? And X, because he had said that he did not like them – they removed the sensation. It was as if he was wrapped in plastic.

Slowly she walked to the bathroom adjoining the little room and the magazine that lay on the bed brushed her thigh as it fell to the floor. Freddie leaned down to pick it up so that the breeze didn't blow it away and placed it carefully on the table, so she would find it when she returned.

The bathroom was between the two rooms of the bungalow that was shared by the four journalists who had been allocated to it. Her toilet bag was on the floor next to the hand basin. She rummaged in it for the Kotex she had bought from the shady looking chemist in Maputo the day before. She had asked for Tampax but he had said, with the horrible leering look that so many men assume when women talk about their bodies and menstruation, that Tampax did not exist in Maputo. Kotex; her mother had used them, plump pouches of cotton between her legs. At least they sold them in Maputo. Imagine washing old bits of waste material like the Victorian girls used to do. She sat down on the toilet, pulling at her underpants while she moved. They hovered around her ankles. She looked down. A bright red splash ran down her leg, nourishment for an unborn child. Oh great, she thought, and with a wet washrag that she took from beside the basin she wiped it away. Bright red blood, it was a beautiful sunset colour. Sighing, she placed the white Kotex pad on her panties, pulled up her jeans and got up. It had looked so good that blood, she was afraid to hide it. Maybe it would go away when she wasn't looking.

Red, like the sky at night, red like the ruby the Indian nurse wore in her nose, red, red...

Freddie read the paragraph again, just to keep the images in her mind. She liked them; it is not often that menstruation is described in a story. Will Self sometimes did it, but only occasionally. Then, as Freddie glanced up to say something, she saw, with a slight shock, because she had really liked the paragraph, that she, her character, was scowling at her. A better word than character? What is a person in a story if not a character; a character, like all of us?

'Why did you have to describe my periods?' she asked Freddie. 'It's not really a subject that I like or that should be written about.'

'Ah, but you don't want to be a washed-out old woman who is no longer fertile,' Freddie replied. 'Society declares that it is sexy to be fertile, an image of youth. Just imagine… I could have got you asking for hormone pills in that chemist for your old used-up body parts. Menopause. Your periods could be finished.'

'I suppose so,' she said, still thinking. And then she pushed her hands through her short dark hair and walked to the door of the bungalow.

She walked outside. Freddie watched her from inside. She could barely see her, the window was so small. A small boy was sitting on a piece of cloth just outside the door. He was playing with a broken piece of wire, trying to fashion it into something that looked like a small animal. Next to him was a sick-looking black and white dog, a sort of Labrador, but not really. It seemed to be constantly scratching itself.

'Hello sweetheart,' she called to him in English. 'What are you doing? That looks so pretty.' The child smiled and, although she knew he could not understand what she had said, he seemed to understand that her words were caring. She walked over to him, crouched down and held out her hand. A little brown hand pushed itself out of the long sleeves of a man's shirt, and reached to touch her. She touched the fingers gently, and said, 'Let's see what it is that you're making, Amil.' She gestured to him at the same time that she spoke so that he would understand. The dog growled, and Amil said something to it that quietened it. He handed her the wire object, a small motionless figure of the dog that lay next to him.

'It's absolutely beautiful,' she said, 'much better looking than the real thing, and at least it can't scratch.' The dog scratched itself again and nibbled at what was probably a tick or a flea in its coat. It whined. She put her hand on the top of the boy's head and turned to walk away. As she turned, Freddie got up and followed her.

Freddie walked next to her. The young boy put his hands down onto the ground and rolled, as if he were a ball, alongside them; the dog pushed its nose underneath his torso as if to help him along. The bandage, which only yesterday had been white, was brown and dirty. It wrapped around his lower body like a fitted sheet that covered a mattress, around and around his small waist, almost up to his chest. Both she and Freddie walked slowly, so that he could keep up with them, this bobbing ball that came up to their knees. As he moved he seemed to be making noises and trying to speak to her. She looked down. He gestured to the bandage that by now was trailing like a bridal veil on the ground. It had come loose.

Oh god, she thought, what can I do? Oh my god. He was whimpering now and the dog whimpered with him. It was as if they were singing together, whimpering in unison, the high notes and the low notes, small sounds of boy and animal. More of the bandage came off and now she could see the raw stumps that that had previously been the top of his thighs. The excess skin that had covered his legs – they had not removed enough of it – hung down into the dust like a pair of trousers. But where were his legs that this skin, this outer leather garment of his, should have been covering? The blood was now running fresh; one drop and then another fell into the sand.

Bright red, red, like the sky at night, red like the ruby the Indian nurse wore in her nose, red, red... Red for the unborn child, the child in uterus, but he had already been born.

She called out to a nurse. 'Kolyani, come quickly. I think we need a new bandage here.'

The nurse with the beige skin and angel face came over, effortlessly lifting the child onto her hip with the words, 'Thanks, I fix it all up now.' Putting her hand to the child's face, the nurse talked soothingly in words that she did not understand. The dog ran along next to the nurse and the boy as they moved off and into the hospital tent.

She turned and moved towards where the other journalists

were. 'I want a whisky,' she said to Freddie. A whisky to dull the pain that had moved from the top of her thighs and into her stomach. And all around the war raged on.

'Play it Sam, for old time's sake, play *As Time Goes By*,' Freddie said quietly to her. 'It's time for the song.'

You must remember this, a kiss is just a kiss, a sigh is just a sigh. It's still the same old story, the fight for love and glory, a case of do or die... The fundamental things of life... No matter what the future brings. As time goes by...

We must get back to the movie.

Yes, she thought, I suppose we must. The words of the song rang in her head, but they seemed to be all wrong. That was not how Sam had sung it, or had he? Sam did not sing the song the way Amil and the scratchy dog had sung it.

She and X had said goodbye at the station. She left for a war, X for whatever war happened in London. Ilsa left for a war hero. How could X know about anything really? But more than this, why did Freddie make her dwell on him so much? There seemed to be so much more to think about.

She sat down in the drinks tent and asked for a whisky. Freddie sat down next to her. She said nothing. There was the sound of a plane overhead. Where was it going to, a promised land far away?

'War is a strange phenomenon, so pointless really. Absurd, this community of violence,' Freddie said to her. 'And if there was no war, do you think that someone would just make one? Maybe they could make a war movie to inspire a war, like *Casablanca*? Wasn't the movie made to inspire the Americans to fight for nothing at all?'

'Is that the kind of thing you think I should say? Moral integrity. Intelligent and analytical, that's what you want, don't you?' she replied. 'But I can't, really I can't. You say it. Be the omniscient narrator or something.'

'We're all just fighting for the biggest nothing in history,' Freddie replied, 'the biggest nothing in history. And of course there must be people who die, people who have no legs, otherwise it would not be a war. We kill to make the war real.'

She thought she heard the sound of a bomb falling – that whistling sound, like bombs falling in the movies. But it was only her imagination, or maybe it was Freddie's. She no longer knew who was doing the thinking, who was thinking for whom, or if anyone was thinking at all. She tried to say something, but Freddie spoke instead.

'Roles must be played in life,' she said, 'and in a war these roles are stark. Villages and towns must be burnt or bombed, bridges must be blown up. We must all continue to play the game. The defeat is apparent here, but it must be made manifest by more dead bodies. There must be mourning by those who love the dead. And what is your duty? Your duty is to tell of the war to others so that they can be shocked or self-righteous, patriotic or filled with angst. Otherwise there would be no point in having the war at all.'

A man sat at a nearby table. He too was drinking a whisky. Strange drink for a Frenchman, she thought, but then maybe there was nothing else to drink except South African beer. He was making a telephone call on his mobile phone. His *haute couture* leather bag lay on the table next to him. He was carefully groomed; clean-shaven and his lips had a glow to them as if he had just applied lipstick.

'Just in case you think there are reception beacons in this area because he's making a call, don't be mistaken,' Freddie said, and simultaneously jotted this down in her notebook. 'These journalists work for sophisticated newspapers, a lot of money has been spent getting them here and ensuring that they communicate with their papers. The media moguls have sent satellites to orbit space. They send e-mail, make long distance calls, send video footage and digital pictures.' She turned to Freddie to reply, but Freddie had already moved off. She was considering the next chapter; she had already moved out of this one.

What now, after all this melodrama? What can I try now?

Anything, I suppose, Freddie thought. After all, in this business who can fail? They're just words. Or is it real? These ever-present questions tormented her as she wrote. She wanted her character to suffer inner turmoil because it is so much more heroic than settling into a life of bourgeois propriety. Suffering is adventurous. It's alluring. But that, of course, is another story, or maybe just another point of view. And these are just words on paper.

An older man walked up to the journalist. He waited patiently while the journalist spoke into his mobile phone. '*Bien, bien.*' Then he ended his conversation, '*Au revoir,*' and turned to the man.

He was dark and slightly better dressed than most of the other refugees in the camp, but not as well dressed as the journalist. He put his hand compassionately on the journalist's shoulder as he bent towards his ear. In a bit of Portuguese and a bit of broken French he said, 'I beg of you, *Monsieur*, watch yourself. Be on your guard. Along with these unhappy refugees come other scum. This place is full of vultures... vultures, vultures everywhere... everywhere.'

The well-groomed French journalist, whose Dolce & Gabbana jeans were bought on the Rue de Rivoli, smiled at this display of concern. '*Merci. Merci, Monsieur,* I thank you for warning me.'

The man smiled and patted the journalist's clean silken shirt. The journalist wiped his lips and took another sip of his whisky. Then he brushed his silky shoulder and reached into his bag for a cigarette. He placed a bright white Gauloise, which he had bought from the duty-free store at Charles de Gaulle airport, between his shiny lips and, with his silver lighter, he created a flame. The flame flickered, the cigarette smoked and he sucked heavily on its white-tipped end. Then he reached into his bag again. His whisky was finished and he wanted another. In the camp they took all currency... Francs, Escudo, Dollars, Pounds. He felt his computer, but he couldn't feel a wallet. He picked up the bag frowning.

'*Merde,*' Freddie heard him curse. But the wallet was

gone. The man who had approached him was nowhere to be seen. The French journalist got up cursing, then he sat down realising that cursing in a foreign language wouldn't help him. Words, any words, wouldn't bring his wallet back. It was an inconvenience, but he could mail Paris for more money tomorrow and borrow from the others while he waited.

And so in Casablanca, we wait, and wait, and wait...

Yes, Freddie thought, I hear you say, 'Ah, I've heard it all before, a pretty story that goes together with the sounds of a tinny piano playing in the parlour downstairs.' But the wow finish, that's what you haven't heard yet. Will you get it, that wow finish? The feeling of standing in the rain with a comical look on your face because your insides have been kicked out. For good or for bad, welcome to the fight. This time, who knows which side will win.

III

On Thursday he received a letter from a friend, or maybe it was an acquaintance, who had left Johannesburg for a land where the earth was whiter than white and the natives were no longer brown but yellow foreigners. 'Can I really say that this person is an outsider as other exiles are outsiders?' Freddie said. 'After all, she's not an exile because she stole the sacred money from the church; she just wanted to be far away from people who were slightly darker than her. She chose a place where the official policy was to feed alcohol to those darker than pale to keep them inchoate. Anyway what did it matter? They were always an amorphous and incoherent set, different to those who were pale. They were "they".'

This person had moved to Sydney, Australia. She had moved away from war and famine. Or so she thought. Had she really moved away from all of this? Didn't the darker aboriginal with the fat of the sheep dripping down his chest, who had been hunted down and killed, come back each night to haunt the white settlers, to haunt her? Didn't the white settlers dream of the *Songlines* and not know of what they were dreaming? And famine? What was it she had said? He tried to remember. Oh yes: 'One of the biggest problems we have here is the sun. You know, it causes immense damage to the skin. It can even kill a person. I wear sunscreen every day, but it's difficult to decide what kind to use.'

A famine... Possible, he thought. Why was she still a friend? Why did she still communicate?

'You are still her friend because I want to write this letter,' Freddie said. 'I like the contents of the letter; it goes well with this chapter. And anyway, I think you might fear not keeping contact. If you communicate somehow with people, you can pretend that you're not alone. And it is always nice to pretend. It makes you feel okay.'

Alone, he thought, I am so alone that I need to read these letters. He lay down on the bed in the bungalow and unfolded the white pages of the letter.

Darling
What are you doing playing around in the war zones? Don't you know that it's plain dangerous. And everything, absolutely everything, is happening here. You just can't believe it. You really should get out of that nowhere place and come to somewhere. That place is a dead end, a dying continent, except for its mineral wealth.

Last night I took in an extremely avant-garde piece of theatre in downtown Sydney. It was the Oedipus myth, the Sophocles story, but a modernised form of it. Oedipus Rex, set in the here and now. You know, globalisation and the alienation of the ordinary person, their exile from the real world of happening things, their relationships etc. It was fantastic. The set design was all done via computer graphics projected onto the back of the stage, strangely three-dimensional. Modern technology is amazing. The boy who played Oedipus was delicious; his head was covered in black dragon-like tattoos. Not that I like tattoos. But no wonder his mother fell in love with him. I mean who wouldn't?

Work is really stimulating. This business research is really taking off in Australia. Investors these days care. They care about the ethics of business. Profits have been put under the spotlight. Investors don't want to be caught with their pants down, so to speak. They don't want to be seen to be participating in anything dirty. I'm making a very real contribution to transformation. Fascinating stuff.

See ya

He looked at the clock on the bedside table. The letter lay next to a glass of water, resting like a confession on the table, a confession of meagreness. He picked it up and read it again. Was this all that they did in Sydney, worry about the rays of the sun? What about love, did no one love anyone in Sydney? Did no one fuck each other and get sexually transmitted diseases? Did no one have violent fantasy sex that others frowned upon but that they did anyway, he wondered.

As he got out of the narrow bed, the water glass fell over, but it did not break. The water glided effortlessly over the letter. The ink ran and stained his fingers black as he tried to rescue the writing. He stroked the wet paper and it felt like the skin on X's chest, wet and sweaty.

This could be a love letter, a *belle lettre* from X, he thought. But it was not. It was a letter about the wonder of another country, another place, outside. He picked it up, crumpled it into a ball and threw it into the dustbin.

'I think the writer of the letter is correct; we must move away from the war zone, for the moment at least,' Freddie thought. 'It's getting altogether too claustrophobic in this camp. I need the sea. Maybe, mmm, let me write about the meeting, X and my character, the meeting at the sea. Let me go back in time, backwards. And something about a family murder... After all, isn't this just what the Oedipus story is, a family murder?'

But she could not really move the story away from the war zone. The story is set in a war. Still, Freddie thought, she wanted to see the sea, so she moved the location to a Maputo guesthouse. Still a war, almost, but also near to the sea – forward to the ocean, backwards in time.

The guesthouse was just down the road from the Casa do Sol – dirty, but with a beautiful view. From the window of his bedroom, if he looked through the bright green palm trees and past the miserable grey shacks on the beach, he could see an endless expanse of turquoise. He could remember every detail of that view, the grey and the blue, and for the sake of certainty the green – although, Freddie told him, green was not in the original script. It was a dress covering the nakedness of the city.

Mrs Pereira owned the guesthouse. Marina, her daughter, a plump sad-looking girl, and Regina, a tall middle-aged black woman who looked as if she could have been beautiful some time in her life, did most of the work. Regina sang as she washed the dishes or did the laundry. She sang words he could not understand. The songs seemed melancholy. Mrs Pereira did not do very much. She was blind. She sat very still in a chair near to the kitchen. There were holes where her eyes should have been, or so he imagined, for the eyelids were closed, drawn down over empty sockets. There was nothing left inside those holes to keep the eyelids open. A space for eyes. A woman who could see everything for only the eyes bring forgetfulness.

He was distracted again. He wondered what it was that he would like to find. Sex, love, a movie that he had seen a while ago, a video in the small burnt-out flat of a friend in Johannesburg. Some French director, what was the name? Ozan? Maybe. A whore from Marseilles who sang the *Marseillaise* while she gave her male customers head. Head in a hole. And no one ever turned on the lights to find out what head was part of what hole. Movies, a distraction. What was it he was thinking about? Sight... seeing... The blindness of the dead, the solitary dead.

It was Regina who saw everything. Regina was always there, close by, watching. What was her story? He was curious. And Mrs Pereira? She never sang the *Marseillaise* for she was Portuguese. But he was exposed to her anyway. The vacancy of eyelessness staring at him.

'Why are you wondering about sex?' Freddie asked.

'It's the weekend soon,' he replied. 'And weekends are the time for sex and familiarity and love. One never thinks these things during the week, Monday to Friday, concentration, work ethics. But on the weekend, time for fun, and what is there here for me this weekend? No sex, no love, nothing.'

'No,' Freddie said, 'love is an illusion – two old people

holding hands together in front of a television screen.' Freddie continued. She had that look on her face, the one she always wore when she was pretending to be erudite. 'Love is always an illusion. We all think we love one another, but the lie is in the kiss that we exchange.'

'Shit,' he mumbled. 'Shit,' he said again. 'Love is not an illusion; I'm not buying into this narrative. And anyway we can't debate this now. Isn't it already part of the story? Anyway, I'm late.' But love wasn't in the story; he just liked to imagine that it was.

The newspaper was beginning to get jumpy. He had to send in a story by noon – anything. They kept on calling him, muttering that he had not sent in anything to grab the readers. Hellmann, the fat editor who moved only from his fortified home in a Johannesburg suburb to his fortified office in another Johannesburg suburb, kept on nagging him. That call yesterday: 'What the hell are you doing up there? It's bloody expensive to keep a foreign correspondent... and the readers want all the gore, they want front-page stuff. Get some blood for us.' More of the same invective. 'No I don't care. I don't give a fuck what the bloody blacks do to each other. But the public wants you to sound as if you care, and I want to sell the fucking newspaper.'

'What did you put that in for?' he asked Freddie. 'You know I can't write. You do the writing. And anyway, I don't know what real blood looks like, what it feels like.'

'But I know what blood looks like,' Freddie said, 'and I am going to make you see it. I am going to make you feel it.'

Dreamily he thought about passion. That was Freddie's word; dreamily. But was it the right word? The look on his face spoke of infatuation, excitement, hunger – not of dreams.

He left the room and walked to the bathroom, which was across the hallway. Jesus, he thought, as he looked into the washbasin, that daughter and her hair. He filled the basin with lukewarm water. Long black strands of hair were everywhere, in the plug hole, under his feet. They stuck to his bare soles like strands of seaweed, or blue bottles more likely, he thought, as the long hair wrapped around his fingers. Quickly he filled the basin. The black hair waved at him from the murky water. He washed his face and shaved. Not that there was all that much hair for him to remove. He was lucky. His beard was not thick. As he ran the razor down his chin he thought of a girl, Marina possibly. A girl's soft skin, black hair. He imagined he could feel her hair on his neck and shoulders. He could feel the rasp of his unshaven face where the skin moved as he pulled the razor downwards. He could feel a girl's cruel hair, or was it a man's, graze his mouth, his chin. He shuddered – anticipation. The razor slipped in his wet fingers and the blade entered his skin. There was a small cut on his cheek, bloody.

Red, like the sky at night, red like the ruby the Indian nurse wore in her nose, red, red…

Freddie, who watched him from the doorway, shuddered too. She wasn't quite sure why. She was there with him in Xai Xai – passion and a man; not passion and Marina – but that part of the story had not yet been written, so she could not know what would happen. Would Freddie even write that part of the story? Maybe she would never know what happened. Maybe she couldn't even imagine it.

After he had finished in the bathroom he walked through to the kitchen. Marina stood at the large stove.

'Coffee?' she asked.

'Yes, and good morning,' he replied. She handed him a cup of steaming coffee. He felt an urge, Mrs Pereira was not in the room, and Freddie had been unrelenting.

'Ask her, ask her,' she kept on saying to him, 'ask her that question, the only question really.'

'Tell me Marina,' he said as he filled the teaspoon with sugar and stirred it into the coffee, 'what happened to your mother's eyes?'

'My mother's eyes? Why do you want to know?' Then

Marina looked furtively at the black woman who stared back at her. 'My mother's eyes,' she repeated. The black woman continued to stare. Her eyes glowed, yellow like a cat hunted in the dark. 'No,' Marina said. 'No,' she said again. She looked angry, or was it sad? He couldn't really tell. She turned away from him and turned on the tap that hung over the sink. The water ran from it freely. He finished drinking his coffee and went back to his room, where he picked up his bag before walking out to the entrance of the house. He walked down the Avenida Julius Nyerere to find a taxi. There was something about those eyes, those yellow eyes of Regina's that drew him inwards, something that could not be made into words.

'How do I describe a city that has been through a war?' Freddie asked him as the taxi drove towards the centre of town.

'You don't,' he replied. 'Use some kind of literary device – allegory or something.'

'Hmmm,' was the sound that Freddie made.

The offices of the Maputo *Daily News* were in the middle of the city. The building was broken down and the windowpanes had bullet holes in them. The editor, a short fat Mozambican, was adamant that he would never replace these panes. 'They are like a memory,' he would say, 'a monument to our struggle, our independence struggle.'

That's it, Freddie thought, I will use something that already exists, a story that someone told to me, to describe this city. The bullet holes, the names of the streets, the broken down buildings. There is a skeleton of a half-built building in Maputo; you may have seen it. They call it *Quattro Stagione*, like the pizza, four seasons. It is built on a piece of dry land; there are no plants or trees surrounding it. Everybody who goes there always asks the same question. Why don't they fix it up? The structure is there. And whomever you ask will give you the same answer; the answer is engraved in memory. The building stands as a memorial to everyone; a statue somewhere in a park, the grave of the unknown soldier.

He had asked this same question of the Mozambican editor.

Freddie had listened in. 'This building is more powerful than any statue or grave. It stands there majestic in its isolation and decay. When the Portuguese left the city they destroyed everything that they could find. This building was under construction. It had not been completed. And when they left they poured cement into the electrical conduits and into the drains so that the building could never be completed. It would have to be completely destroyed and rebuilt. And we will not do that. So now it stands as a memory.'

'Like this story is a memory,' he said to Freddie. 'But whose memory?'

And the years will go by, Freddie thought, and the story will be told so many times. I am telling it to you even. And I wonder if anyone ever remembers what happened, or whether they just remember the words that they use to tell the story. And does it make any difference?

The building that housed the newspaper was ramshackle, but its outside appearance belied what was inside. For a poor newspaper with a small local circulation it was surprisingly well resourced. The Russians probably, he thought as he walked. Upstairs was an old movie theatre with lines of chairs bound to the cement floor. They could not be moved. The purple velvet of the seats collected dust and the germs of decay. Behind the seats was a projector. An old movie looped its way through the slits and the holes. Around it were tins, the lids decorated with spiky spirals. Some were shut, others open. Negatives, coloured and black and white, oozed onto the slime of the floor. Orson Welles and rosebuds. The man who worked the projector sat at the doorway, waiting for the theatre to open and the people to arrive. It never did open and the only people who sat in the chairs were the stars of the films waiting to be shown, waiting for an audience.

He walked down the stairs to the basement where the archives were. He had to write a story before noon, but he wanted to explore the archived film first. He wanted to watch a movie, silent and still. Why, what was it in those yellow eyes?

Momentarily he thought about the civil war in the north, a new war, pointless in its way, but ongoing nonetheless. And Freddie kept reminding him of it. She frequently wrote about him in the wasteland of the refugee camps. He sat down at the computer and for about an hour he stared at old newspaper cuttings that had been scanned into a microfiche. Then he saw it. A picture of Regina stared out at him. She glowed in the light of the machine. Her eyes were blue. The headline screamed (the short little editor's style), '*FAMILY VIOLENCE – TRAGEDY OR JUST DESERTS*'. So overdone, that headline. It was dated five years ago dessert, just after Independence Day. The names of the roads had not yet been changed.

'*An eye witness account of Portuguese history,*' was the byline. Freddie looked over his shoulder as he read on. She too was curious. '*At a shop on Avenida Bastinado a man was stabbed to death in what looks like a revenge killing. A young boy, the son of a domestic worker, stabbed and killed Carlos Pereira, a local Portuguese shop owner. At approximately 7.30am, the boy, who was employed by Pereira in his shop, for no apparent reason, walked up to Pereira with one of the gaffs that were used to slice up the fish for the day's sales.*

The boy then repeatedly stabbed the shop owner in the stomach. Not satisfied with this gruesome killing, the boy then proceeded to disembowel Pereira. He then hung up the shop owner's intestines on the fishhooks and carried on with the day's business. Some say that Pereira's intestines were even purchased and eaten by customers who knew no better.'

Oh my god, Freddie thought, the intestines were purchased, and eaten. Not for dessert though, I suppose.

They continued to read. '*In an interview at the Pereira home, the domestic worker, Regina, said that Pereira was a cruel man. He had regularly beaten and raped her, but she was afraid to do anything about it, fearing that if she did she would lose her employment. And she was devoted to Joana Pereira, the wife of the deceased, who was also regularly abused by her husband.*

Pereira was the father of Regina's son, Carlos Junior. While Pereira refused to acknowledge the child as his own for fear of being excommunicated from the Portuguese community, he nevertheless gave him a job working in the shop. It was this boy, his own son, who had killed him. But there is more to this hideous event. While the story was being told by Regina, screams were heard. We ran to where the sounds were coming from.

In the kitchen of the home, Mrs Joana Pereira held a serrated knife to her face. There appeared to be blood running from her eyes. And then, as we came closer, we saw that the Portuguese woman had put out her own eyes with the knife. She was screaming and confused, but she appeared to be saying, "I never knew, I never saw anything. I should have seen, I could have seen."

Shortly after this the boy was taken into custody and Mrs Pereira was rushed to a nearby hospital. There her eyes were fully removed. They could not be saved.'

He looked further and found another story that told of the event. The facts were substantially the same. His guesthouse, the blind woman and Marina, Regina, the domestic worker – he could see them all in front of him, convicts lined up against the blue background of the glowing microfiche. She had put out her own eyes, forever culpable for what she had not seen. And now she would only see the memory that she remembered, the memory that she created. She could never forget. He felt as if he were a witness to a Greek tragedy. This was not real life; it was a play or a novel.

'Well it is a novel,' Freddie reminded him, 'but it's fine, you can still feel shock.'

He gulped in damp, hot air. The room was strangling him. He turned the machine off and went outside. The sun was shining and he thought he could see the blue ocean peeping out from between some palm trees. Blind forever – forever culpable for what she had not seen.

And he – well, the story was already written, for even though the events had happened long ago, they would still titillate the readers of his Johannesburg newspaper. And after the story? He closed his eyes so that he too could no longer see. Blind, noble blindness, like that of a Greek statue. Let Freddie do the rest of the thinking and seeing. He was tired now.

Was he in a movie? It's all just a game, he thought. What was Freddie doing making him stay here? She must surely do something soon; maybe he could meet someone – a titillation.

But, as he thought this he felt like a man who was trying to convince himself of something he did not believe. He wanted to believe in this game, he wanted to love, to believe in a truth. The story had its own momentum. He could do nothing about it, and if he really wanted to know what would happen he could just watch the movie. It was all there. Freddie was in control of his destiny. Still, he couldn't help wondering, if he had a destiny.

IV

She could remember the picture so clearly, or could she? How many times had she replayed it? They met each other quite fortuitously. X was in Maputo – in the city for a few days only. He was on his way to the coast, to one of the few resorts that were still open. It was Friday. She had walked into the bar at the Costa do Sol, La Belle Aurore. It was slightly run down but the name, being French, seemed to give it an air of Parisian bohemian sophistication. A trick of the mind. The illusion of words that make up a name. As she walked inside the bar, she wondered why the name was French rather than Portuguese.

She had intended to stop in the bar for just a few minutes before going back to the Pereira guesthouse. It was hot inside the bar and the drapes that covered the windows made the space feel oppressive. It was as if all who sat there had just been put to bed, and were now drifting off sluggishly into a world of nightmares. Everybody was covered by a dim violet hue, the colour that occurs just before you drift into sleep, the dark purple of sleep.

A man who looked as if he had been in the sun too long sat at a beat up piano, in a photograph, sepia.

'Play it, Sam. For old time's sake, play *As Time Goes By*,' Freddie said quietly. 'It's time for this song.'

You must remember this, a kiss is just a kiss, a sigh is just a sigh. It's still the same old story, the fight for love and glory, a case of do or die... the fundamental things of life... No matter what the future brings. As time goes by.

The words of the song rang in her head. She had heard them before and she knew that she would hear them again. But they seemed to be all wrong. That was not how Sam had sung it, or had he? Was this the café in Montmartre, the same café, or was she somewhere else?

Her jeans clung to her thighs, sticky with the sweat of the day and her palms felt clammy. She wondered if it was the heat or the story of the Pereira family she had just telexed off to the newspaper that made her feel so uncomfortable, sweaty, afraid. She had changed the dates so that the readers of the newspaper would think that the event had just occurred. Now she needed a long, cool gin and tonic.

It's for the malaria, she thought with a smile, and remembered her Mozambican colleague laughingly telling her that she would have to drink enough tonic water to fill the whole of the Indian Ocean if the quinine was to have any effect.

She walked over to the bar. 'A gin and tonic, please,' she asked the barman. He had an earring in his right ear. He was a knife thrower in his spare time. He had a long scar that coursed down his right cheek ending at the top of his throat. I wonder if he also throws knives at people and if they throw them back at him, she thought. She knew him well enough by now to know that his rudimentary English covered the words 'gin and tonic'.

Without words he poured the drink and handed it to her. His long slender fingers, pale at the ends where his nails were, briefly touched her hand as she took the cool glass from him, and he smiled. 'Two hundred.' She handed him the money, taking care not to touch his fingers this time. They were somehow too long, too attractive, sexy. They had felt so much.

'Your bag, it is falling off your shoulder. Careful, you may lose it,' Freddie said to her.

She moved her hand to her bag and pushed the strap back onto her bare shoulder, her skin, moist and slippery from the heat. She walked outside onto the terrace where she could see the sea. Freddie walked next to her. 'On a clear day you can see forever,' she whispered, half to herself, half to Freddie, 'forever and ever and ever.' She sat down and put the bag beside her. Then she leaned down and took out her cigarettes, small brown rolled cigarillos that you could buy in the market at the stall that also sold cashew nuts, salted or unsalted, whichever way you wanted them. She lit the cigarette and blew the smoke out across the long veranda. It floated above the air looking for somewhere to land, like an aeroplane above a landing strip.

Suddenly she heard a great crash. Freddie jumped up. She just sat there. Someone was sprawled out on the sandstone floor next to her table. Splinters of glass lay like magnets on the floor ready to pierce the skin of anyone who was careless enough not to be wearing shoes. There was a puddle of foam, all that was left of a beer.

'Fuck!' she heard. 'Fuck it, look what you've done.'

'Me?' she said indignantly. What had she done? She was just sitting there minding her own business. 'Me?' she said again, incredulous.

'Yes, you!' this person replied. 'Why the hell did you leave your bag in the middle of the floor? I suppose you wanted me to trip over it.'

And then they both burst out laughing. X (she learnt that this was the name of the sprawling figure) got up off the floor and put out a hand, then he took it back. 'Better not put beer all over you,' X said, wiping his hand on the back of his khaki trousers. 'I'm X.'

'I suppose I'd better buy you another beer,' she said. She was still laughing.

X looked absurd. His neat, but just-creased-in-the-right-places trousers had a dark stain on them, right across the top of his balls, which she could now see clearly outlined beneath the wet clinging material. She could even tell that he was circumcised. 'I think that that would be appropriate,' X replied, 'and I think you'll have to clean these trousers for me. They are the only ones that I have and I'm still here another day or so. Can't go out looking like this, can I?'

She looked at his balls again. 'I think you can go out like that,' she replied, knowing that he never would. X would never participate in a wet trouser competition.

She walked back inside the bar and asked the barman for a Singa, the local Mozambican beer. She wondered how the hotel maintained its constant supply of alcohol in the war.

'It's the South Africans,' Freddie had told her when she asked this same question. 'They bring everything in, guns and alcohol.'

The barman handed her the bottle, and then, she could not be certain, but she was sure that his index finger had curled around her hand as he handed it to her. His finger touch was light and feathery, a shudder passed between her thighs. When she returned to the veranda she saw that X was seated at her table.

'Oh well,' she thought, 'I can do with some company. The only person I seem to speak to these days is Freddie – and sometimes Marina.'

But Freddie was no longer at the table, she was sitting on the ledge that surrounded the veranda, watching them. Freddie looked at X a little more closely. Dark brown hair, a pleasant smile. Not Humphrey Bogart, she thought, but then a remake is never quite the same, especially if it is in colour.

X seemed to talk about everything that night; what he was doing in Maputo (on holiday in fact), what he wanted in life, his London life, his hopes and dreams... He even talked about food. X liked to cook. She didn't, and that was all she told him. Freddie sat quietly wishing that she had a notebook on her. How would she remember this one-sided conversation? But then, on the other hand, why would she need to? If she wanted to, she could write it up anyway, but even that she didn't feel like doing today. And she knew that it was all a lie. A magnificent lie. It was the heat, it made her feel lethargic. And talk, talk is so dull, especially talk about life and love and hope and dreams and cooking.

Stay with the images, Freddie thought as she watched them speak.

And so Freddie watched. The sea made a murmuring noise

in the background. A blue-black butterfly with delicate pink-veined wings settled on the red hibiscus that grew in the pot just below the stairs of the veranda. Its wings moved ever so slightly. Freddie couldn't tell whether it was the quick breeze or a conscious attempt by the beautiful insect to steady itself on the petal. Now it inserted its long rolled-up tongue into the centre of the flower, deep, far away. She could feel and taste the nectar that it sucked upwards.

A small child with deep-set brown eyes that bored into her walked below the ledge. He put out his hand to ask for money. His white shirt fluttered in the wind, like a pennant, a peace call, a sign of surrender. Freddie watched him watching her. She would not give him money. How could she really? What real difference would it make to him, this small gift that he begged for? And then he was bored of waiting for his gift. His fingers closed over the blue-black wings of the butterfly. He held it between his thumb and forefinger, aloft, a trophy. With his other hand he slowly squeezed its body, yellow mucus oozing from the insect's mouth following the line of its curled up tongue. The sweet nectar that it had recently taken from the flower was spat out. Then the boy dropped the butterfly on the ground and moved off. Maybe he was just going home. The butterfly moved its wings slowly, and then it was still.

And soon the moon began to rise over the grey water. It played over the waves. Sometimes it rose and sometimes it fell. Its light lingered on the butterfly, and then moved on. And only Freddie noticed these small details.

After what seemed like forever Freddie came over to the table. 'We should go,' Freddie said to her. 'I'm tired. But don't worry, there can be a lot more of these conversations if you want them. I don't really like conversations, but if you want me to give you time for them while I write about other things I will.'

'Oh well, I'd better go,' she said. 'I have lots of things that I still need to do before the morning.'

'Well, I suppose I must also get my stuff together. I want to be off early,' X replied. 'But let's talk sometime. I don't want to never see you again.'

'Yes,' she replied.

'Wait, I'm going to stay at this beach place for the next couple of days,' X said. He wrote the name of the hotel on a square of white paper and handed it to her. It is on the coast, just north of Xai Xai. 'Come and meet me there.'

She turned and walked across the long cool flagstones. Of all the gin joints in the world he had to trip over her bag in this one. She turned to Freddie as they walked side by side out of the hotel. 'Why did you put him in here? Things were just moving along at their own pace. I don't need this emotional entanglement. In fact, I would prefer to be alone. Alone with thoughts of Marina's soft, girlish skin.'

'Well, I want someone real in your life, otherwise the story won't work,' Freddie replied. 'And it may as well be X, so I think he's here to stay, for a while at least.'

The moon rose higher as they walked down the street. Small clouds scudded across the sky, sometimes in front of this silver orb, sometimes to its side. The miracle of this light in the darkness of no electricity showed them the way. The roof of a shanty rose up into the clear dark air and the green and yellow creeper that grew up and between the rutted corrugated iron pieces covered the metal, decorating the handiwork of its builder. A black cat ran in front of them and slunk into the drain. A lone palm tree swayed in the sea breeze. Time seemed to stand still for a brief moment in this inconsequential story, just two people walking along a road. And the clouds moved again and a breeze blew in the sounds of the sea.

V

She packed a small over-shoulder bag. She did not need much; a few shirts and an extra pair of jeans, a box of rubbery condoms. She looked at the box. 'Rough Riders' were the words on the one side. On the other, the same words were written in Afrikaans. Afrikaans, she thought as she looked at the writing, a misshapen language in this city, one that no one knows or speaks.

Condoms were difficult to find in Maputo, much like tampons. She had bought them the last time she was in Johannesburg. At the time that she'd bought them she hadn't known why she put them in the chemist basket, but she had done so anyway. Now she would need them.

'Glad that you kept that box,' said Freddie. 'I told you, you may need them and that you should keep them, remember?'

As she had taken the box from her bag with the intention of throwing them away Freddie had stopped her. 'You never know,' Freddie had said. 'You may need them in the future.'

What future? she had thought. Future is just another word for today, another word for yesterday. Fashion conscious journalists and red, dusty war refugees. But she had kept the condoms anyway. The box was not very big; it was easy to slip into her wash bag.

'I also have a few books,' she said. 'That's why this pack seems to be so heavy.'

'Yes, I forget you are a book lover, rather than a movie lover,' Freddie said. 'A letter lover. You sometimes even use the words of others in your stories – a double crosser.'

With the bag on her shoulders she walked out of the guesthouse and down the Avenida Julius Nyerere. She walked towards the bus station. A four- or five-hour bus ride to Xai Xai.

Freddie walked beside her down the street. 'Strange how this city grows into your skin,' she said as they walked. 'It is a hot and dusty city. Only some of the roads are tarred. There is the occasional open sewer and often a city map does not accurately reflect the myriad changing streets.'

'I think that it is the simple things that delight me,' she replied. 'The coffee shop where I buy the black, strong, fresh coffee and eat the fresh butter-filled croissants. I watch the woman behind the counter grind the black beans. And then, as I put my lips to the chipped edges of the china cup, I stare at the old men who sit there hour after hour reading yesterday's newspaper that is filled with today's news. More coffee, more words, more of the newspaper stories where only the names and the places change. Maybe it is the lilting warmth of the voices that speak a language that I barely understand but that, although there is a war on, has no tone of animosity or aggression. Maybe it is the very new white Land Rover that I know has been stolen from someone in Johannesburg and secretly brought over the border. It stands on a street that is not tarred and is parked right next to a pothole. It is the white goat accompanied by a kid that wanders across my vision and sniffs the new wheels, then in a desultory fashion turns to nibble on a banana skin that is lying on the street. And as I bend my head over my book, I can smell the faint hum of the fragrance of frangipani flowers. And then, when I look up, I see the fast-flying humming birds that point their long beaks into open yellow blossoms. I think that all the dying have created a life here, a musical life in which people live and die, and they laugh throughout both these experiences. I laugh too, do you?'

'That was a long descriptive speech,' Freddie said. 'I am impressed with the way that you have with words. Anyway, to answer your question, I laugh or I cry, and neither of these two activities makes any difference. To speak of laughter or tears is simply to give different names to the same illusion.'

Freddie wondered where she had read the words of this long speech before. Was it in a travel essay in a Johannesburg newspaper? The description had a tone of unreality to it, the romance of someone who does not know what it is like to die in this city. The sound of someone who will always remain outside of it, always just observing and never experiencing.

'Well, I don't mind what you think of my words,' she said. 'I think that they sound as if I am in love. My imagination is a tourist's imagination, and why shouldn't it be? I am in love with a place, and I am in love with a person who is in this place. I have a home.'

She walked onwards. Then the bus station was in front of her. She remembered reading a guidebook that was published when Maputo was called Lorenzo Marques and smiled as she remembered the words. *Air-conditioned buses run on the hour. They are clean and comfortable and always on time. Lorenzo Marques has buses that you can rely on.*' Now the book was out of date. There were no air-conditioned buses anymore and the vehicles that did exist did not run on the hour. The buses were just a way for people in the city to travel somewhere else. They were no longer recommended to the tourist, so the tourist no longer travelled on them.

Near to the bus station she stopped and looked around her. 'This space is a mixture of a nightmare and a wild wonderful dream,' she said to Freddie.

On her left stood a group of soldiers. There must have been at least six of them leaning against a wall and murmuring. She looked at them. Their fresh army uniforms were clean and ironed – Russian fatigues, a blend of bush colours. But this is not the bush, she thought. This is a city. And Russia is covered in snow. The soldiers did not blend into their surroundings. Instead they stood out, green trees against the pitted, brown-coloured brick wall that some time ago had been white. A feral tortoiseshell-coloured dog ran between the feet of one of the soldiers. He looked at it. He lifted his boot upwards and moved his leg forward. The kick was quick and hard. His boot landed on the dog's back. The dog did not know where the blow came from and how it got there. The small animal seemed to fly through the air. Then it landed close to where she and Freddie stood. It let out a small cry, almost a whimper, and then it rose from where it had landed and limped away. It had not been able to take the chicken bone that lay near the soldier's feet; it had not been able to get close enough to grab it. The chicken bone remained where it was, cold. The dog lay down and licked the blood from the cut, which the soldier's boot had made in its rusty torn fur.

There was dust everywhere. She imagined that if a person was walking, and there were many who did this, the dust would cover them in that fine red sand that somehow, despite bathing, would never leave them. The dust clouds shone through the sun as it gathered around the heads of the people that walked. She watched the soldier who had kicked the dog. He took out a small mirror and looked at his reflection. She wondered if the soldier thought of this dust as well and imagined it settling in his beard. The mirror was small, the size of an orange. On the back of it was a flower with five petals indented. A black 'Mary Quant' flower in Maputo. The Mary Quant fashion shop in London, in the rain, far away.

Freddie pointed towards the end of the street. 'That,' she said, 'is one of the best restaurants in Maputo.' She pointed at a restaurant that had a Chinese sign – maybe it was its name – hanging on the awning that covered the veranda. In daylight it had a bedraggled look, but she could imagine the lights at night. The Chinese lanterns swung in the breeze. They seemed to be simultaneously beautiful and tawdry, cold and exotic. On the steps stood a woman. She was wearing nightclub clothes, sequins glittering in the sunlight. She wondered if Freddie could smell her perfume. Maybe it smelt like an angel. From inside came the sound of voices and music. There was no one who was Chinese around the building. A picture of Mao hung above the sign. He had slanting eyes and yellow skin.

She sat down on a wooden bench. Suddenly she felt the presence of something crawling. She looked at a bag that lay on the red ground next to her. It was neither her bag nor

Freddie's. It belonged to a man who sat alone. Some sandshoes were tied by their shoelaces to the handle of the bag. Then she noticed a small hand alight on the handle of the suitcase, the small fingers were in the incipient stages of trying to untie the shoelaces. The man seemed not to look; he just stared sideways at a woman who was sitting at the corner of the bus station. She was watching him closely, staring into his eyes. She noticed how he kept watching the woman, while simultaneously, from the corner of his eye, he watched the hand. Then he let out a bellow, the hand was whipped away, a flash of colours moved quickly into the dust of the street and settled down under the skirts of the woman. The man winked at her and leant down to retie the sandshoes to the handle of his suitcase. The corner of his eye had not betrayed him, not this time.

Freddie looked at the soldiers as they leaned into the wall. One of them looked down the barrel of his machine gun. It was an AK47, a new and modern edition of this weapon. 'Modernity,' said Freddie, 'if this is what I must call it. What is a better word for what the new Western half of the world – although not all of it is in the West – has imposed upon people who are different? Civilisation, maybe – except that this word really means anyone who is Greek. And not everyone is Greek, so civilisation can't have been successfully imposed. Technology, maybe – the guns and the bullets are a product of technology. And yet they destroy, they kill, and technology is supposed, if we are to believe all that we read, to enhance people's lives. Maybe death does enhance life. Maybe that is why guns are sacred. Efficiency – my portable computer makes me efficient. I can write a thought. Then, if I do not like it, I can just erase it. I do not need to start the page all over again or use a lead pencil to make this thought appear or disappear. The thought can be expunged in a minute. But there are no computers in this bus station. Only the journalists and the United Nations and the well-intentioned industry aid workers have computers and mobile telephones. And the shops. They are supposed to create convenience. You can walk into a supermarket and buy ready-cooked meals and chicken pieces with no blood on them, fresh vegetables that you believe have just been picked from a vegetable garden. You can even buy fruit juice that has preservatives in it so that the sell-by date is drawn out. Yet here there are none of these shops.'

'Do I have to listen to this?' she said.

'You don't have to,' Freddie said. 'Many people, when they read a book, just skip over those parts that they find indefensible or trite; they read only the parts that they like. But I will go on anyway as I feel like putting this down. Remember when we stopped to watch the soldiers shooting at the scarecrow targets? I thought about how people have given up a part of themselves for this slice of modernity. We have brought it to them and handed them a small piece of it. And if they have not wanted it we have forced it onto them. And now they want this Western world, now they want to push their world and culture behind them as if it is backward and retrogressive. There has been more than just the eradication of culture, family, religion and community. There has been the eradication of the spirit, a defeat of the soul. They want to be like us. And yet... and yet it is all so ill fitting, this modernisation, so ill fitting that it almost seems as if people are saying, maybe quietly, fuck it, fuck you.'

'Stop,' she said. 'I want to get on a bus. I'm more concerned as to whether I will be able to find a bus to take me to Xai Xai. Tell me something beautiful. Tell me about the colours in the crowds, the women in bright cloth, the yellow bananas and pineapples. That man in the corner playing his flute. Listen to the sounds – they roll through the air like a vial of perfume that has tipped over and now permeates the sky.'

She walked up to the wooden table where an officious man sat. In front of him was a piece of paper and he held a pen between the index finger and thumb of his left hand. 'When will the bus go?' she asked him.

'At nine o'clock,' he replied. His mouth was crammed with bread and the thick gravy of the cow – or maybe it was the goat – that was in the plate in front of him, ran raggedly down his fingers over the pen and across his thick wide mouth. He leaned forward so that the liquid gravy would fall into the plate and not onto the white paper. 'Would you like some food, this food?' He laughed as he watched her sigh. They both knew that the bus would not leave at nine o'clock; she would have to wait and wait.

And so in Casablanca they wait... and wait... and wait...

Freddie sat down next to a man who wore only a long, ragged shirt and green underpants. The underpants were new and freshly laundered. The man was boiling a small kettle on a burner and the coals glowed. 'I think if we are going to have to wait I should drink some of this tea,' Freddie said.

'Yes,' she replied, 'I think I want some as well. I prefer this African tea to the saccharine taste of Coca Cola, and it makes me feel less thirsty in the sun. I like the bitter harshness of its taste. What is it made from?'

'It is made from green tea that is boiled forever on a small burner,' said Freddie. 'And because it has been boiling for so long, it is strong. And the sugar has etched itself into the hot liquid because of the flames. Drink some of it. It will make you feel good. It has an hallucinogenic effect to it.' Freddie turned to the man. 'Can we buy some of your tea, please?' she said.

She held the cup between her hands. She felt her fingers burn. 'I wish we did not have to wait so long. I want to get there. I want to get onto the bus so that at least I can feel myself moving closer to X.'

'Soon, very soon the bus will leave. And you will be on it,' Freddie said. 'Don't worry. I know that X will still be there when you get to Xai Xai.' Freddie sipped her tea from the tin. It had a torn picture of olives on the one side of it. They were as green as the tea was.

She turned to listen to the man who played the silver tarnished flute. He played onwards, the notes rising in the humid air. They drifted forward. Forward towards the modern world. Forward to a world of money and fiscal policy and economics. Forward to the loss of a part of his world. The privilege of being part of a great equality, the equality of hell, and there was no exit.

At 11 o'clock she rose and went to the man at the wooden desk. 'When will the bus come?' she asked.

'At 12 o'clock,' he replied. 'Just sleep.'

'Stop thinking about time,' Freddie said. 'Stop being influenced by what is only an arbitrary division in a day. It is a pernicious and *bourgeois* instrument; don't keep imposing it upon yourself. An African city has no time. We are fixated with time. "Are we going to be late? Time is money. Why is it taking so long? What is the delay?" At least here there is some resistance to this imposition; things always run late, often very late, sometimes not at all.'

'I suppose that I should not ask these questions in this bus station,' she replied. 'I suppose I should just eat the fruit and drink the African tea just like everyone else.' She sighed and looked around her. The man who had sold them the tea decided that it was too hot to stay awake. He lay down and gently fell asleep on the mat next to her feet. His breath rose and fell in his thin brown chest that was covered in hard curled hair. The flies settled on his eyes and mouth, but he did not stir.

'He is used to movement,' said Freddie. 'Not the movement of time.'

At two o'clock she climbed onto the bus and sat on the melting plastic seat. A woman sat next to her. 'She can't be more than thirty years of age,' she said to Freddie, 'but she looks older. Years of child bearing, the sun, lack of proper nutrition have taken their toll on her. Yet she is dressed in oranges, reds, greens and blues.'

'She is saying to all of us that her body is something to decorate and that she is proud of it,' Freddie said.

In fluent English the woman turned to her and said: 'Where are you from?'

'South Africa,' she said.

A smile lit up the woman's gnarled face. She leant over and touched the skin on her cheek and said, 'African.'

Freddie smiled at the scene. 'Yes,' she said, 'you can feel ashamed if you want to. After all, you are privileged by colour, and yet she can speak to you in English. She probably only has a few years of schooling in a remote village far away.'

She leaned her head back and closed her eyes. It was a long road.

VI

He took the backpack off his back. The straps had dug themselves into his skin – a whip. His shoulders were covered in welts. He had been travelling for four hours on the potholed road. He felt the holes in his bruised skin. There was no space in the bus to put down his bag. The bus was full, full of Maputo, the women and the children and the chickens; the men had all gone to fight in a war. On the roof several goats lay in the sun and bleated. Their noses were burnt and red. The road meandered inland, through green and brown – green where people still tried to grow vegetables, brown where the fields were still charred from the scorching rained down by whoever the enemy was. But neither the discomfort nor the heat could make him forget X, the outline of his balls on his khaki pants where the beer had fallen. At the Xai Xai bus station he had found a taxi, the one taxi that still circled the town. The driver turned the key but the engine would not start. Then he leaned down and joined the two loose wires that hung from under the steering wheel. The engine shrugged into sound. It was anguished sound. For another ten kilometres he felt the holes of the road again, but now all they seemed to do was to caress his cock. The bruises they caused were different now. They hurt, but he wanted this hurt. The taxi stopped in front of a building. He opened an unsteady door and got out. The sweat dripped from under his arms. Then the car continued moving. It was the wrong guesthouse. This one was barricaded up. He was hot and angry. He walked down the hill, the whip lines on his shoulders stinging as his sweat rolled into them. Now he stood outside the door to bungalow number 18, hesitant. Even if the phone lines had worked, he wouldn't have called to say that he was coming here. Now he was uncertain. What would X think, a stranger arriving on his doorstep?

'You can pretend to take control,' Freddie said to him. 'It will be okay. When have I ever let you down?' But I will let you down, Freddie thought. I have to; otherwise there won't be a story.

He raised his hand and knocked softly on the wooden door. The door was open and moved inwards as he knocked. He couldn't see X, but he knew that he was in the room. He could smell him – that faint smell of urine that all men seemed to have hovering around them. Then he saw the shadow reflected in the brown-spotted mirror of the open cupboard door. The reflection beckoned him inwards. Like a corpse, the body moved slightly as the breeze from outside blew the cupboard door. It swung inwards, the blank holes that were closed eyes gaped upwards. X's mouth was slightly open, his bare, smooth chest rose and fell with his breathing. His nipples were wine stained, darker than the rest of his skin, bullet scars, and his hands were flung behind his head as if he had just fallen backwards. He walked into the room and moved up to the body. Slowly he leant over it and took one of the nipples between his lips. X moaned, as if in a dream. Then the cupboard door swung shut and he could no longer see the image, nor feel the nipple in his mouth.

'Hello,' he said and walked over to the bed. He leaned over to kiss X. Lips lightly on a cheek.

The guesthouse was one of the old guesthouses. There were no people staying there. Only the foolish and the brave came to this coastline in the war. 'What was X?' Freddie wondered. 'One of the brave or one of the foolish?' Or had she already decided this? He was the only guest in Xai Xai.

The bungalows were in a state of disrepair. The man and the woman who ran the place were age-old hippies from somewhere in America. They still believed that they were in Washington protesting against napalm in a jungle they had never seen.

They still vigorously opposed the austerity plans for the poor, plans designed to make young men become soldiers because soldiers, dead or alive, earned a salary. The guesthouse was their focus group, a forum in which to discuss burn wounds and sweatshops. Here they could still protest, if only to themselves, against a war. They were safe, as no one could hear them. They were imbued with a mild domestic psychosis, this pair of Americans. Their eyes were in limbo. Stasis had set in. All around them an African war raged. And all around the war the world lived in a cloud of spiritual lassitude. It drew down its window blinds when things were not what it wanted to see. And the window blinds in Xai Xai were always drawn down as it was too hot to keep them open.

But it was their faces that made Freddie look at them. The faces of this out-of-place couple seemed to be asking a constant, powerful question. 'What now?' they seemed to say to each other. 'What now?' they seemed to say to their guests. 'What now?' they seemed to say every time Freddie walked past them. And nature crept into the house. It rested on the old buildings, burying the work of those that built them, and the couple could no longer defend this insurrection or have their question answered.

The line of the sea was beautiful. It reached up and met the sky in an ever-present palate of blue. Small white terns with yellow legs that had escaped being eaten by hungry soldiers waded on the sand, their long black beaks forever digging deeper for hapless snails and other life forms that lived under the shoreline. Blue bottles rode the waves. Freddie walked by herself today. It was one of those days which could either develop into a storm, one of those storms that shocked the bones out of a person's body, or could clear so she would be able to watch the sun sink down below the horizon. An African sunset is always more beautiful than a sunset anywhere else, she thought. But that is only because the dust particles are thrown up into the air by the chaos below. That is only because the smoke of the guns spread out into the atmosphere causing the sun's rays to split and diversify and scatter. She felt alone in this vast space and humbled by a gigantic universe over which she had no control. It could take her and fling her upward in a storm or it could allow her to sit peacefully watching the sun's painting. She could only control those she had left behind in the humid close cabin. I had better get back, she thought, back to the comfort of two people and a controlled space.

But they were not in the cabin. They walked quickly along the beach. Freddie saw them in the distance, two figures silhouetted against the dark grey sky. God had chosen to bring the storm today. The clouds gathered behind them, dwarfing the two insignificant figures. Now and again a roll of thunder sounded its horn. It was still far away, but moving in closer. Raindrops the size of small pebbles were starting to fall. A drop of water fell on Freddie's arm and lay there like a diamond gleaming in the dusky light. Freddie put her tongue to it and tasted the cold stillness. And now these drops were moving downwards more quickly. Another and then another fell on her shoulder and on her breasts, and she just stood there.

In front of Freddie the two figures started to move faster, to run before the coming of the storm, pitting their feeble bodies against the raindrops.

In the cabin X lit a candle; the generator was not working tonight. X pulled him close. Side by side they sat at the table, a bottle of Evian water next to the whisky. He did not feel like drinking whisky now. He felt like lying in X's arms. X's arms gave him comfort; they made him feel small, just like the storm made him feel small. 'My watch has stopped,' he said to X. 'I wonder what time it is. I wonder what they are doing right now in Johannesburg? I guess they are asleep in America, and waking up in China.'

'Who are you really?' X asked him. 'Who are you, and what did you do before, what do you do now, and what do you really think? Why are you here?'

He put the index finger of his left hand on X's lips. 'We said no questions.' A smile played over his face. His lips puckered, grotesque in the candlelight. He looked across at Freddie who was leafing through a picture book, an old book with a collection of pictures from *Life* magazine.

'I can't tell you that now,' Freddie said in reply to his questioning frown. 'I can't reply to that now because I don't know who you are. And I don't know if I ever will know. And remember that I am a writer; I have a taste for the secret. If there is no secret there will be no book. More than that, I fear characters who are transparent, who have no room for a secret – characters that demand that their whole life be marched out in the public square. No internal space left for the reader is a sign of the totalitarianism of freedom. Everything available for everybody. Lies and silence are the only subversion.'

He looked at Freddie. What did she mean? What was she trying to explain to him? Was this the something about moral integrity that she often threw at him, sideways, when he least expected it, or when he least wanted it? He walked over to where Freddie sat, and looked over her shoulder at the pictures in the book. 'But I do want to know who I am,' he said.

Freddie turned over a page in the picture book. 'Look.' She pointed at the picture – an old black-and-white photograph of Ingrid Bergman and Humphrey Bogart. 'Just imagine; you could be in a movie and then you would know exactly who you are. In a movie there is no secret.'

The thunder rolled around the cabin as he walked back to the table. He put out his hand. X took it gently.

'It sounds so much like gunfire, canons in the distance. I know that it's the thunder, but maybe it is also my heart beating. Kiss me quickly,' he went on. 'Kiss me as if it were the last time.'

X did not reply. How could he? X did not know that there were other lines in that scene for him to say. He put his hand on X's cheek and leant forward. Then he kissed X. 'Here's looking at you kid,' he whispered. He knew those lines by heart now. He could finish the wide-angled scene.

Sometime later after they had gone to bed Freddie watched

them. The storm continued, but it was slower now. Gleams of noiseless lightning dropped into the room through the cracks in the curtains and lingered on the now still bodies as if looking for something, like a spotlight. It picked out the bodies and then moved on to the pieces of still furniture; a chair, a table, the empty whisky bottle. It moved to the scattered clothes on the floor. Slow drumbeats of thunder beat time against the walls of the cabin, knocking, knocking to come in. Outside Freddie could hear the waves. The once peaceful water now lashed the land. She closed the picture book. Bogart and Bergman could now get along with their own lives, away from her eyes and her preconceptions. Freddie felt as small as a pygmy. She felt inessential – not that pygmy's were inessential – but she liked the metaphor, in the vast space that was the world.

'Play it Sam, for old times' sake. Play *As Time Goes By*,' Freddie said quietly to no one. 'It's time for this song.'

You must remember this, a kiss is just a kiss, a sigh is just a sigh. It's still the same old story, the fight for love and glory, a case of do or die... the fundamental things of life... No matter what the future brings. As time goes by.

The four days that they were together passed quickly. And he believed that he learned a lot about X. But Freddie knew that he had learnt nothing. The only truth that he learnt was the feel of X's body, and even that was no more real than celluloid. What he learnt was a lie, a fabrication, a physical presence. And, Freddie thought, you will only know this later.

VII

X, the Good, walked though the shopping centre. And why do I describe him as good, Freddie wondered as she wrote the words. Well, I suppose he is good, she thought. Good in the way that we want people to be good. Good to look at with his dark hair. Good, as he is paid an average salary every month by someone else. Good, as he keeps to his watch; he goes to his office every morning at eight and leaves it at five. Full time employment so that he can fill in all his time. His work is dull, but he thinks that it stimulates him. Good in all the ways that the world wants you to be good. X is good with a capital G.

X walked into the building. It was a large supermarket, the kind that sells everything from coffee to lawnmowers. A Johannesburg city supermarket. The market in Maputo was very different to this supermarket. The sounds were different. Here there was the sound of the refrigerators. They hummed. There was the sound of the air conditioners. They hummed. There was the sound of people's voices. They hummed. The chickens were footless and frozen. They did not cluck, neither did they scream for god's mercy as their heads were carved from their bodies with a blunt blade. The dogs at the supermarket entrance were chained up outside on specially built dog-chain poles. They did not bark. They did not rush through your legs as you walked on by. They put their excrement decorously in one small patch. At this supermarket there were no sounds of a bargain. The noise, as X walked in, seemed to call him – the drone of people, ordinary people who were doing their shopping. Nescafé, Tampax, Kellogg's Cornflakes, the voices said. And if X stopped moving down the long aisle, the voices did not stop.

A family that was made up of 4.6 people stood opposite the cereals – one wife, one husband and 2.6 children. 'What do you think we should get?' The wife turned to the husband who was with her.

'I think Cornflakes,' he replied. 'They say that they are good for the kids. The writing on the box says that it has 56 per cent of the recommended daily roughage allowance in it, and it has all of the necessary vitamins and minerals.' He looked at his 2.6 children. One of them walked beside him, the other sat in the seating place especially made for children that was built into the trolley's wired structure. The 0.6 child could not be seen.

I wonder if it is a he or a she, thought Freddie, or maybe it is just a part of my statistical market imagination. The walking child, a boy, stared at the cereals vacantly. He grabbed at a box on the shelf.

'I want this... I want this...' he said, and pointed at another kind of cereal. 'It says that you get a free Superman picture with it and in some of the boxes there is even a plastic Superman. Wow! I want Superman.'

The woman took a packet of Cornflakes off the shelf. It had no plastic Superman in it. 'It is a great price,' she said. 'Let's get at least five boxes.' The man turned to the child who had fallen to his knees. The child prayed. Let's get out of here. Freddie thought she could read the child's mind. Let's get out of here, god. Please god, take me out of here so I can do something I think is meaningful. I want to have an adventure. I want Superman. I want to be Superman. I am Superman.

But, thought Freddie as she wrote, there is only nausea. And you, you poor little person, will never get out of this vomit. All you are is alive. 'But then, maybe I am wrong. Superman is meaningful and Superman is alive. Well sort of alive. A cripple in a wheelchair and he cannot speak. But... maybe he can fly.

'Yes, take five of the boxes,' the man said. 'We can save R5.50. Look.' He showed the woman some numbers on a calculator. It was a pocket-size calculator, one that fits so easily into the pocket of a husband's trousers.

The woman took the calculator from him and pressed some of the buttons. She was checking his figures, checking as to whether he had calculated the numbers correctly. 'No, I think we can save even more,' she said. 'I calculate a saving of R6.50.' She took five packets of the cereal off the shelf and put them in the trolley next to the child who sat there silently.

The child in the trolley smells bad, thought Freddie. Maybe he has soiled his diapers. They had better buy those super-drying nappies as well. I have seen the advertisement for this brand on television. In it there are two children, one who cries and one who does not. The one that cries does not wear this special kind of nappy so they must make a child think he is happy. I wonder if I should show them the shelf on which they are kept.

X passed the checkout counters, tall and dark as he pushed the trolley. A woman who was very old was paying for her load of supermarket goods. 'What?' he heard her say. 'Don't try to cheat me, girl, these tampons are on special offer. Don't overcharge me. I want to speak to the manager.'

Freddie glanced at the old woman and wondered why she was buying tampons. She is too old to menstruate, Freddie thought, but these days, who knows? Maybe hormones in a pill have genetically engineered her to keep on menstruating. Maybe she just wants to stay young, and what better way than to be reminded of your youth once a month? The cold dark blood of youth.

Bright red, red, like the sky at night, red like the ruby the Indian nurse wore in her nose, red, red... Red for the unborn child, the child in utero, but he had already been born.

X felt in his pocket and pulled out the list. Chicken, dental floss, milk... he read. He reached into his jacket and took out a pen so that he could mark off all the things that he intended to buy once he had found them on the shelves and put them in the trolley. X liked lists. Lists comforted him. Lists organised him.

Up and down the aisles. First it was the toiletries. He put the dental floss in the trolley and then thought that maybe they needed toothpaste as well. So he took the peppermint-flavoured tube that was next to a can of the deodorant that he liked. The toothpaste tube had writing on the side of it that said, 'Guaranteed – No Cavities'. X had no cavities. He went to the dentist regularly. He did not need deodorant, so he did not take a can of it. 'Never anything that you do not need,' was his motto. Then he walked to the aisle where the breakfast cereals were neatly stacked. They all looked healthy. Muesli with bran and nuts. Cornflakes. Oatmeal. He reached over and took the Cornflakes off the shelf. 'Might as well take them,' said Freddie. 'They are, after all, good for a healthy life, and the price is great. They contain 56 per cent of the recommended daily roughage allowance, and you can save. I cannot remember what the husband in that family told his wife, but I do remember that he said that you could save.'

Then the milk. Fresh or long life, he wondered. Freddie tapped him on the shoulder. 'Long life,' she said. 'You have a short and prosaic life ahead of you.' X put the long-life milk into the trolley. At the meat counter he stared. There was a peculiar smell at the fridge. Decaying and cloying, as if someone had recently died and the flesh were only now beginning to rot. 'It is the smell of death,' Freddie said to him. 'It smells like Amil's arm, or maybe a princess in her grave.'

'The meat is packaged so well,' said X. 'I can't tell what it is – a sheep's shoulder, a piece of the filleted backbone of a cow, chicken wings...'

'Well, I suppose that they are not going package Diana's corpse. It would be irreverence. And Amil's legs, they won't be vacuum packed,' said Freddie. 'They were blown into a thousand pieces. Difficult to find all of them. These cellophane-wrapped pieces of sheep and chicken seem a whole lot easier. Sanitised, clean, no superfluous fat, no washing the dust off them needed.' As X leaned over to put the chicken wings in the trolley he wondered what it would be like to fly. For a brief moment Freddie allowed him to think fantastically. The sense of absolute freedom that wings allow, soaring above the earth below... Then X's reverie was interrupted. That was a close call, thought Freddie. What on earth would I have written next if I had to get X to imagine being able to fly? A woman brushed against him. She was middle aged, but she looked younger, or so X thought. Her diamond earrings glittered in the tawdry light. The gold on her wrists spun round as if it was woven onto her. She too took two packages of chicken wings and then moved on. X felt his cock move in his trousers.

X frowned. Lines appeared on his forehead. Ah, dog bones, he thought, and picked up a packet of assorted white-knuckled bones. As he put them in the trolley he thought about Xai Xai. But it was a fleeting thought, only a moment. He thought about the bones of her spine, a lover's spine, hard and covered in soft human skin. Then he looked at his shopping list. Everything was neatly crossed out. Everything seemed to have been acquired. And he would not get more than what was required; after all he was a hard-working man, parsimonious with his money.

Mean, thought Freddie, mean. But I suppose I have to dress up the writing with long and interesting words. And 'parsimonious' could mean anything. It is not as commonplace as 'mean'. It does not have that critical edge to it. She frowned. I couldn't make him buy sex. He is mean. X would not spend money on sex. I suppose there was free sex, but that is part of the story. Or was it just gratuitous, the sex part? Sex makes a reader read on just in case they find some more of it in the words. Just a hint of sex makes a reader think that they will soon be reading the real thing. Soon they will taste it. And anyway, X did not buy sex because this is not a smutty story. Readers frown on those who buy sex. I wonder why? We all buy it in some or another form.

X walked towards the checkout area. He stepped over a mop and broom. Someone was cleaning the floor. He looked down at the woman. Her uniform was red and white, contrasting with the harsh yellow neon light of the supermarket. The handle of the mop stuck out from the bucket. He moved it aside, as there was no space for the trolley to pass. She looked up at him. Her eyes said that she was bored and weary. Her eyes said she could not give a fuck about clean floors and mops and obstacles in the path of oncoming trolleys. At the checkout counter there was a queue of people – shoppers in a Johannesburg shop buying groceries, buying what was needed to sustain them in their daily mundane lives. He leant against the trolley and looked at his watch. Thank god the supermarkets stay open after working hours, was all he thought. Now it was his turn. 'Click click click,' went the buttons of the till. The thick but effective fingers of the woman took his goods one by one and rung them up.

'Two hundred rand and fifty-five cents,' was all she said when she had finished. He took out his wallet and paid her the exact amount – blood money. Then he pushed the trolley out through the revolving doors to his car. He loaded the bags into the boot. As he looked up he saw the silhouette of a security guard on the roof of the supermarket. The black figure stretched out over the world. The man held a submachine gun. It was pointed at X's chest. X wondered why he thought about a machine gun pointing at him in this parking lot. His heart bent towards the excitement of Xai Xai.

'I may make you die,' said Freddie.

X shrugged; maybe I have thoughts of mortality on my mind because of all those death and mutilation stories from Mozambique. He did not think about sex. He thought about a gun. Then he got into the car and drove away.

X lived in a suburb. He drove into his driveway. The gates opened effortlessly as he pressed the remote-control button. In the dark the house looked like a ship come in to port. It stood there, white and motionless. It was silent and there were no lights on. X sighed. He knew that Y, his wife, was at home. He knew that Y had been at home all day as she had called in to work that morning to say that she was sick. Y worked for an advertising company and they all knew what calling in sick meant. It meant that whomever it was that made the call had had a hard night before that morning. X knew that Y had

had a hard night. She had started out at home with one line of cocaine, but he had seen her put all her paraphernalia in her bag. Then she had said that she had to go to a work function, some sort of cocktail party, and that he should not worry about her. And he hadn't. Y had come home late that night. X was already asleep in the bed that used to be the bed that they shared. Now, most nights, although she would be there lying next to him, he shared it with himself. It would be nice to say he shared it with his dreams, but X did not dream. He was too banal to dream. He just lay there and thought about all the things he would have to do the next day at work. Organise the sound system for a computer company that was giving a presentation to their clients. A meeting of a board of directors somewhere who needed a video conference at the same time. Some of their colleagues were in America. Well, he would have to manage it all together. And then he fell asleep. No dreams of Maputo, no dreams of Xai Xai, just sleep. He even breathed heavily when he slept, heavily and evenly.

Is Y more interesting than X, wondered Freddie. If I make her interesting will this detract from my protagonist? If I make Y interesting I'll make the drug world interesting, and that has been done so many times before – a cliché. She looked at the computer screen and squinted. The screen saver clicked on. A hallucinogenic hazy image of floating windows appeared before her. The drug world – at least one changes consciousness by choice, she thought. You have to pay for it. I wonder if Bill Gates takes hallucinogenic drugs. I wonder if he changes his consciousness by choice. He must do if he makes these windows loom out so large at me. Should I write about how I envy those who knowingly change their consciousness, lose control and leave home? No, I can't get sidetracked into that right now, and anyway there is no Leonardo DiCaprio starring in this movie.

X walked into the house and switched on the lights. Y lay on the couch. He could see the muted scenes of the television as they played out in front of her. She always watched television;

she had nothing else to think about except the quiet killings of the thrillers that flashed across the screen. Blood and torn out throats. 'Hi,' X said, and walked over to kiss her.

'Don't kiss me,' she said as she turned her head sideways. 'I haven't had a bath and I feel like shit and I smell like shit.' She smiled as she thought of the sex that she smelled of – nameless erotic sex, sex for money. X's lips grazed her hair. It was yellow, lank and greasy. Tired hair.

Not such a good line, but I will put it in anyway, thought Freddie. Drugged hair is always tired, tired of the staleness of life.

Why does she have to do this to herself, X thought. Why? What does the drug have that I do not? It is not as if our life is not good. Great new house, newly painted, a domestic servant, a watered garden, even a dog. X bent down to pat the Labrador that jumped at him as he walked into the kitchen. It was not a black Labrador. It was golden. 'Come boy,' he whistled after he called. 'Come, I have something for you.' The dog was already nosing at the bags. He knew that somewhere in there, there was something for him. X opened the fridge and put the long-life milk inside it. A blast of cold air reached up and penetrated his eyes.

Noble eyes, wondered Freddie. No, I won't give him noble eyes. His eyes are not those of a Greek statue. X has ignorant passive eyes. Blind, yet he can still see. Did you know that in a drowning the eyes are the first go, she mused. Empty eye sockets through which the fish swim. Shall I give him empty eye sockets? Shall I make him sing the *Marseillaise*?

X put the cut-up chicken in the freezer. Then he unpacked the dry groceries. He put them in the cupboards, neat rows of Marmite and cereal and salt. He shook his head as he saw a square of yellow cheese, unwrapped, lying on the kitchen counter. Couldn't Y have put it away, he thought and frowned. In this heat cheese goes off and I bought it only a few days ago. Last of all he took the bones out of the plastic shopping bag. The dog barked happily as X opened the back door and swung a bone through the air onto the green, grassy, mown earth.

The golden dog ran to it and started gnawing. X walked back into the sitting room and looked at Y. She looked back at him. Her eyes were more noble than X's eyes. They were vacant, glazed over, insalubrious – the eyes of a Greek statue that were not there.

'Have to go out,' Y said to X. 'Can't stay in another second. I've been here all day. Why don't you come with me? We could have fun. And you can see a bit of what is not your life.' Y winked, one noble eyelid closed. X looked at her. He knew that all she really wanted to do was to get some more cocaine; she seemed to depend upon it nowadays. 'Come,' Y continued. 'It isn't often that a woman has the chance to play before her husband. I can play the hero. What do you think?' And she laughed.

No more heroes, Freddie thought. I've described enough of them. Enough of Che, or was it Castro that I wrote about. Enough of Lumumba. Y depends upon her powder and that is heroic enough for this story. Freddie looked at X's neatly combed hair and pretty khaki trousers. She depends upon it so that she can forget about the neat creases in X's trousers. All a hero wants is to find a way out of the world. That is why they die so well and so dramatically.

'All your salary goes on that noxious white powder,' X said to her. 'I hate it. I hate that white powder that you put up your nose or put into a pipe to smoke.' His voice was emotive. 'Don't you sometimes wonder if it is worth all of this? I mean, what are you doing it for?'

'Shall I remain here hiding out with you then?' Y said to him. 'Or shall I carry on the best I can in these circumstances? If I stop the powder it will be as if I have stopped breathing. I shall die. If we were all like you the whole world would die.' She lit a cigarette.

Freddie looked at her. Strange, she thought, X is a man who has convinced himself of something that he absolutely believes in. I suppose each of us has a destiny, for good or for evil. Good destinies, evil destinies, one good, one evil, one simply the absence of the other. The destiny of X and the destiny of

Y, for good or for evil?

'I wonder if you know that you are trying to escape from yourself,' X continued. 'And of course you will never succeed.'

'You seem to know all about my destiny,' Y replied.

'And I know more than either of you,' Freddie said. 'I know for instance that X is in love with the sex that he had with a woman, or was it a man? I know that it is strange that I too am in love with this same man or woman. I know that Y will remain in this world. There is nobody to blame. There is no explanation. And what of it anyway?'

'Come on,' Y said. Now her voice was soft and cajoling. 'You need something a bit more interesting than the space-age technology you deal with day in day out. It's not a stand-in for actual communication. Don't think of me only as a person who sniffs cocaine. I am also a human being. And I can tell you something different. I can tell you about sweet sentimental families and money,' she laughed.

But X needed to spend his money on groceries. And he needed to save his money for a time when he grew old. 'Maybe you won't need money for when you are old,' Freddie said. 'I don't have enough time. A day is very short and I don't think that I can write so many words. You will never be old. I will never be able to get there for you.'

'No,' X said. 'Can't. Got to get up early tomorrow. Have to set up a presentation for someone.' He walked over to Y. 'Don't go,' he said. 'I feel like staying here with you tonight.'

'You don't really want to spend any time with your wife,' said Freddie. 'What you really want to do is masturbate and fuck someone.'

'No, I want to go,' Y replied. 'I want to feel the night. I want to touch the music and the buzz. I want to see the smells of the tortured.' She turned to go to the bathroom. Freddie looked over at X as he sat down on the settee. Y also turned to look at him. Y almost felt sorry for him as he sighed.

'Yes,' Freddie thought, 'pity him. It's okay to pity him. I'm not trying to make him an object of pity, but not is a word that I forgot to delete.'

X heard the shower, water gushing down her hard spine. He thought about Xai Xai and the storm that night. I never really knew her, or did I, he thought. Actually, I never really wanted to know her. And he laughed to himself as he thought about how he had exaggerated his life – his life in London. I suppose she never knew me either, he mused. Do you need to know someone to have sex with them? Probably not. And he remembered the storm and the *Life* magazine and the sex. He remembered the sex.

X looked towards the bathroom. The sounds of the shower continued. He got up and walked into the toilet. He pulled at the zip of his pretty khaki trousers and thought about her small hard breasts as they pressed against his thighs. They could have been a boy's breasts they were so small. He thought about her face; looking down, all he could see was the dark cropped hair and a moving head that stirred his cock. He could smell her as she took him in her mouth, wet and warm. Sharp teeth that did not bite. A rich tongue. She was skilled at sucking a cock. It was almost as if she knew what it felt like, as if she had done this to herself. She knew what she needed to find. He remembered pushing his cock into her throat, so far back that it touched her vocal cords. She could not speak. He felt her tongue lick at his balls. He remembered the feeling of slackness that came over him as he quickly came to a climax. His semen spurting into her mouth, she swallowed it. Some of the viscous opaque custard liquid dripped out of the corners of her mouth and fell down her chin. She wiped it away with the back of her hand. Then she licked the hand. More of the taste. More of that sweet smell – honey. And still she did not speak. She just licked her hand.

X moved his hand on his cock, up and down, up and down, up and down until he could no longer focus on the white toilet wall. His cock jutted outwards, almost touching the toilet handle. His one hand pushed against the white wall. His breath came in short bursts and then he emptied himself into the well of water. Quickly he flushed the semen away. There should be no trace of him left. Then he took a sheet of toilet paper and wiped the rim of the seat. No trace.

'But there is a spot, a spot of semen on those perfect, pristine, neatly ironed trousers,' Freddie said.

X looked down, and then he dabbed at the spot with his index finger. The domestic servant will wash it off, he thought.

He walked back into the room where the television was still turned on. A newsreader spoke in monosyllables. Something about burning a person in a township. X turned off the sound and watched the image. The burning rubber around a neck. The flames and the smoke. He smelt the burning flesh and saw the filleted spine, half frying in the flames. She had said so little about herself. But what did he want to know. All he wanted was a body – a body for him to do with what he wanted to do. Something that he could possess. All he wanted was to feel her thighs around his waist, and he had felt them. All he wanted was a voice, not a conversation. X sat back on the couch until he heard the water being turned off in the shower.

Better make some supper, X thought. I need to eat, need to be okay so that I can manage work tomorrow. He got up and walked into the kitchen and boiled some peas and baked some chicken. He did not fry the chicken. Too much oil was not good for his cholesterol.

X, the Good, ate his meal alone. Why am I writing this, Freddie thought as she looked at him using his fork to put the peas into his mouth. Why is he even in here, and will anyone ever stop to think and ask? And will Y just keep looking out forever, or will she suddenly someday realise that she is no longer looking but waiting?

VIII

The room was quiet. The room was dark. X, the Good, slept, almost peacefully. Now and again his face moved into an expression, a grimace. It looked as if a sticky plaster were being torn off it. Pain. And then the peaceful expression came again. Peace, thought Freddie, the sleep of the peaceful. Peaceful with a capital P. Maybe X should be X, the Peaceful?

There was a movement outside the front door of the house. A short black skirt and a white T-shirt walked up to the small copper-plated button that was the doorbell. Y pushed it violently The sound of a bell moved inside the house. It crashed into the white pristine walls. X heard this sound. He heard it as if it was a dream, but he knew that it could not be a dream. He did not dream. There was a smash; a figure ran down what must have been a road.

X called to it. He asked it to stop. For god's sake stop. If you don't stop you will crush me. I will lie in the street like Achilles, the slain warrior, and I don't want to lie in the street. I don't want to look as if I am dead because I am dead already.

Dead is exactly what you are, Freddie thought as she wrote the words. A dead person. A dead dream. Some words on a page. Except, I suppose, for those short minutes of ecstasy, those short bursts of pain – not your pain, but the pain of the man you were with. Dead and blind. I wonder; would you have used the image of Achilles? For X had never read *The Iliad*.

X woke up. He felt a bead of sweat gather in the waistband of his pyjamas. He felt the salty water move between his balls. A bubble of sweat trickled downward towards his cock, which was thrusting outwards. X wiped his face and touched his cock. It was hard. Strange, the boy had the face of a girl, and then the face of a boy again. The face that hovered above his stomach, the hands that touched him in places that had not been touched before were a boy's hands. X trembled for Achilles had loved Patroklos.

'You fool,' Freddie said as she looked at him, 'you poor good fool.'

The figure in his mind careered down the maybe road. Then there was a sound in his head. He sat up. The doorbell peeled again; or rather it rang, for it was an electric doorbell. X climbed out of the bed. He dragged on a pair of shorts and went to the door. Y stood there. X could smell her from where she stood in the entrance. She smelt of blended whisky and vomit. Around her wrist was a small hand towel that was covered in blood.

'Forgot my keys,' she said. She saw X look at the towel. 'It's nothing, just a small cut,' she said. 'I had to get through a window.' She pushed past X and walked into the kitchen. 'The cops were running about, they were everywhere.' Y laughed. Y always laughed.

X looked and saw her reflection in the hard neon light that she switched on at the entrance to the room. 'Fuck,' she said, 'what a night. And they all, all of them, the people, they look so great. They appear so great. Wonder if they think? Suppose they must think if they are there and not safe at home in bed,' she continued to speak. 'Suppose they must think if they want to burst your bubble, your self righteous bubble.' She moved a piece of her yellow hair from her eyes.

Yes, thought Freddie, maybe you can see. Even if you are frightened by what you see outside you do not remain hiding in this house. Hiding in the safety of X. You must carry on the best you can in this war of attrition, this domestic war. The dog barked a golden sound.

'One more,' Y said, and took a packet from her bag – a clear plastic packet. She unwrapped the crinkled wrapper as if it were a chocolate bar. She was careful. She carefully poured the white powder, incandescent and ephemeral, into a thin line on the kitchen counter. She took her purse from her bag. Out of the purse she took a fifty rand note. She curled it into a long roll and leant over the white powder. The air from her nostril forced it to move up the roll of money and into her nose. Her hair moved with the air that burrowed into her face. 'Go back to bed,' she said. 'I can't bear to see you looking so fucking self-righteous. What the fuck are drugs anyway, except to be taken? Stop being big fucking brother.' Y looked down at his shorts and saw his jutting cock. She moved closer to him. She touched him hard, caught his cock between her fingers. Then she twisted her hand and laughed. X bent forward in pain and watched her as she turned away. 'You are so fucking wholesome, all sentiment. Fuck off,' she said quietly.

X turned around. Out of the corner of his eye he looked at her. He saw her take out more money from her purse. Then more money from the pocket of her skirt. The telephone rang. X moved to answer it. 'No,' she said, 'I will.' X looked at his watch. It was 3am. She answered the ringing sound. Yes, yes, yes, was all he heard. Then she put the phone down. She came back to the kitchen. 'If I am going to be doing this,' she said, 'it is bloody hard work. But I suppose I earn more than what I did before. Oh, by the way, I now only work in the afternoon. It's easier. Sleep in the morning.' She laughed again. 'Come with me, come to Hillbrow. A customer waits for me.' X shook his head. She picked up her black bag and went to the door. 'Bye,' she said to him. 'Keep sleeping.'

X moved slowly backwards and into the bedroom. Why do I stay with her, he wondered.

'Maybe I can sell the story to you,' Freddie said to X. 'It must be that childhood memory. Two ten year olds running along the beach. Yellow hair flying next to black hair in the wind. Pebbles rasping against your feet as you run with her. The same cause. The same fight. And a memory, for a memory will always be so much better than the experience really was. It will always be more than what happened. You remember something as beautiful, but you must be wrong. Remember it anyway.' Freddie looked at X as she spoke, but all he did was yawn. 'I suppose you're only thinking of yourself now,' Freddie continued. X got back into bed.

'Oh, you mendacious fool,' said Freddie. 'One woman has hurt you and you take your revenge on the rest of the world. Your Xai Xai revenge. You're a coward and a weakling. I wonder what I should do with you. When I wrote about you before, in the earlier chapters, I wanted to create someone whom I could admire. A dishonest admiration. I had to create someone whom I could admire as my character loved you. And I wanted the reader to love you too. I wanted my reader to hold your hand. And now? I knew it all along, I knew that you would turn into this pathetic caricature, a parody. The lover is pathetic. What a cliché. The lover must die now.'

X put his hands behind his head as he lay on the bed. He thinks he has power, Freddie thought. He knows that Y will not leave him. Her past was too good for her to risk thinking about it again. It was too secure, too warm. She wants both worlds. The red stars of blood on the Hillbrow streets. X, the security of the mundane, food and a roof. I have made her want all of this.

But all X thought was that maybe one day, one day Y would know what was best for her. She would want him. He was best for her. But now he wanted the boy's body. He wanted to push his finger deep into that bracken sweet-smelling salubrious arse. He wanted to see his semen run down thighs and catch itself in the faded hairs that trapped it. He wanted to see him look at the magazine and wonder what he was thinking.

'Well you're no longer in Xai Xai,' Freddie said, 'but you can remember it.' X was in Johannesburg and he had to go to work in the morning. 'It is morning already,' Freddie said to him. 'You had better sleep for soon you will have to get up and make yourself breakfast.'

How did I do it in Xai Xai, he wondered as he tried to fall asleep. But Freddie had already written the words and X had already created a picture from these words. They could not, or would not, be deleted.

'You did it because I wanted you to do it,' Freddie said in response to his question. 'And Xai Xai is in my computer hard drive. It is not in you, you who lie in this four-walled room trying to sleep. I have the words, and I have the memory.'

But still X did not sleep. Xai Xai was not real, he thought. It was as if it was a movie and I was playing a role. I even spoke as if I was in a movie. I did things that I would never do in real life.

'Well, I wrote about you in Xai Xai,' said Freddie. 'Okay, you were different to this description, but I wanted you to be different. I wanted you to be Bergman. Maybe you don't look like she did – how could you? She was beautiful in that black-and-white way. Maybe you just have the same sort of nose.'

'Maybe I never even went to Xai Xai. Maybe this memory is of something that never happened,' X said.

'It never did happen,' said Freddie. 'I just wanted it to happen so I wrote it down. And anyway, so what if you've told the story to yourself over and over again. What are memories? If they happened, they did. If they didn't happen, well, so what – you can pretend that they did. You can remember the words that you use to describe the place. You can remember the words that you use to make up the story.'

X is a banal man, thought Freddie. But at least he has me to create a memory for him. And my memory of what happened in Xai Xai is not banal. I suppose I am subjective, but what the hell. X in Xai Xai was almost exciting.

X drifted into a sleep. And he thought of a boy, or was it a girl?

IX

'Meeting in Johannesburg regarding war in Mozambique.' She read those seven words again. The telegram was terse, abrupt in its anticipation. Fuck it, she thought to herself. I can't just rush off out of here because they want me to. I don't want to go. But I suppose they are paying me. She held the cigarette between the first and second fingers of her right hand. With the other hand she touched her breast. Underneath the thin cotton shirt she could feel her nipple. It changed shape as she thought about X. She put her index finger into her cunt; between her thighs she could feel the sticky moisture. Strange that she had these thoughts when her job may have been in jeopardy, but what did she care?

'X hasn't even written to you,' Freddie said. She knew that he had not done so because if he had she would have written these letters. And Freddie wanted to remind her of this.

'I know that,' she said to Freddie. And to herself she thought, yet I think about him all the time.

Freddie looked up from where she sat. She too held a cigarette. 'You have to go to Johannesburg,' Freddie said as if anticipating her next question. 'It is part of the story, part of the plot.' And she knew that she had no choice. Freddie would choose for her. It was all a game, words for others to consume as and when they pleased. 'I suppose I can also cover that Amnesty conference about the people who are held as prisoners by the apartheid government. It is called *Prisoners of the Reich* and it's being held in Johannesburg,' she said. 'That's a good enough reason to get out of here for a few days.'

The taxi wheezed its way to the airport. Like an old man who has emphysema, it could barely breathe. She could barely breathe. She had left a lot earlier than she needed to, as she knew that journeys in Maputo were difficult to control. No one ever knew what would happen along the road. The flight to Johannesburg, just a one-hour journey, could take many more hours than the distance justified. The taxi jerked to a stop. She looked up to see a row of dark figures silhouetted against the fires of the city – an automatic rifle, bayonet at the one end, outlined against the smoke like an erotic sculpture. In some pristine London gallery this image would have won an award. The caption might say something like, 'an expression of post modernism'. She looked at Freddie, but could only see the whites of her eyes as she stared into the distance. There was no fear in her expression, as Freddie knew that this was not real. But how could she know this? She was in the taxi; she could not anticipate what would happen next. The taxi driver said something in Portuguese, which she could not make out. Was it the fear that made him mumble, or just that she could not understand the language well enough to pick up all its nuances?

A soldier stood next to the car window. The taxi driver cursed as he pulled at the handle trying to move the pane of glass downwards. It was stuck and he needed all his strength. His fingers curled over the top of the glass as he tried to pull down the pane. But it would not move. Her window was not stuck. Quickly she turned the handle and it opened. She said something, something like, 'here, it's open', but not before the young soldier had forced his bayonet through the glass pane of the driver's window. It smashed into the glass easily as if it were moving through flesh, but there was more noise than the slicing of flesh would make. A knife through flesh makes a slow hissing sound. As it moves blood will ooze and squelch. It is not a hard sound. It is melodious. But this was loud. Glass is more resilient than flesh, and it shatters, it does not quietly separate. A fragment hit her cheek. She could feel where it cut into her skin. She did not move. Shards of glass. Visible and invisible. The melody of blood as it dripped slowly down her face.

The blood felt like X's semen, a stain on her face. It dripped downwards. Semen, the texture of blood. Semen that made her bleed. The taxi driver was covered in the shattered glass; it fell like sand onto his pink shirt and glowed in his black hair. The young soldier moved closer, the jagged glass marking his face with black shadows. He could not be more than eighteen years of age. He still had the stain of his mother's milk around his mouth where much later in life his hair would grow. Now this space was soft and clean. His hand that held the rifle shook, and his finger that gripped the trigger trembled.

Freddie sat back in her seat and watched. Strange, Freddie thought, what a rifle does to a boy. Take it away and what have you got? No more power. Nothing. Just ordinary things like fear and hurt and hunger.

The soldier's breath seemed to reach into the car, foetid, like decaying meat that has been left in the sun to rot. The soldier was gesturing and pointing at them and the taxi driver was explaining the purpose of the journey. This she could understand. Every now and again the boy would look around at his comrade soldiers as if he needed them to affirm that what he was doing was right. How could he know? How would they know? The rules were undefined. The taxi driver seemed to be pleading now; it was about money.

Up until now she had said nothing, and then with no movements she said to the driver, 'Tell him that we will give it to him. I have dollars, but I must get them. They are in my bag. Tell him that I am opening my bag for dollars, not for a gun.'

The driver spoke quickly; she could see the boy jerk his head in acknowledgement of the request. 'Get out!' he shouted. 'Get out so that I can see you.' Another soldier – he was older than his colleague – moved out from behind the razorwire roadblock. He said something inaudible to the young soldier. He walked over to the taxi and leaned forward. He pushed his arm through the open window and touched her on the face. It was a gentle touch, the touch of power, the terrifying spectacle of power. As his fingers drew down her cheekbone she could feel the liquid blood where the shard of glass had settled in her skin. The soldier took his finger away and looked at the red stain. He slowly licked the blood from a finger that was surrounded by a silver wedding band and smiled.

Bright red, red, like the sky at night, red like the ruby the Indian nurse wore in her nose, red, red... Red for the unborn child soldier.

She reached into her bag and took out her purse, her passport nestled in the safety of a grey satin lining. 'Get out, get out!' the soldier screamed. Slowly she opened the car door and moved her legs out on to the tarmac. She stood upright. She counted the dollars, green monopoly money. What could it buy in America? Not very much, but here it was enough. She put out her hand, the money between her fingers.

'Give! Give!' the young soldier called as he moved from the window of the car to where she stood. The point of the bayonet pricked her throat. One small movement and it could cut deeply, very deeply into the jugular vein. She handed over the money, the paper clinging to her sweaty hand, reluctant to be released. The soldier grabbed it and moved off.

She got back into the car and the taxi driver laughed. 'You are not used to this life, hey?' he said. On his face was a smile, a smile of relief? She could not tell. He must have experienced this many times before, but how could she know what he was thinking? But Freddie knew his thoughts. The taxi driver was thinking about his girlfriend. He thought an ordinary thought; her pretty face, her black eyes and the sex that he had had the night before. And the sex that he had had the night before in her low wooden bed was not as ordinary as the words that made up his thoughts.

'And now you must give me too,' he said to her as he started the car.

Freddie sat in the back seat watching the scene unfold. She looked at Freddie. How could she be so calm? What had she

END

experienced that this did not make her afraid? 'How can you feel nothing?' she said to Freddie. Her voice rose upward as she asked the question, its notes high, verging on the hysterical. She could feel her hands shaking. She could feel tears well up in her eyes.

'I knew what would happen,' was all Freddie said. 'I knew that nothing would happen. You were not put here to become a heroine. This is not a tragedy. There is a real and bigger tragedy out there that cannot touch either you or me. And so I was not afraid. And anyway, it's only my words and I have written enough about heroes. Well, I hope that I have written enough about them to keep the novel on the bookstore shelves – at least for a while; maybe even a book club or two.'

But it felt real, she thought to herself. Her throat was tight and her eyes burned. And the car moved onwards into the night. The upright bodies of the soldiers disappeared into the dark air. No one knew why they were there and no one even bothered to find out. They were just there, dark shadows in the night. Young men with guns in their hands. Part of a photograph of a war.

They drove past the mural commemorating the revolution. The spotlight – the only one in Maputo – shone down on the bold reds and blues and yellows. Faces contorted in grimaces, smiles that emerged from a grave. Samora Machel looked handsome and menacing, his cheekbones glinting in the headlights of the taxi. Russian revolutionary iconography, a cultural miasma, a seething city where little bits of the cold war of the East meets the hot war of the West meets Africa. In the light, the mural glowed grotesquely. It made her feel afraid. It was almost as if she did not know where she was going. The faces in the mural followed her.

'Don't worry,' said Freddie. 'It's okay. It's all part of an adventure, an adventure that you will never experience again, unless of course you watch the movie.' But she was so distracted and so anxious that she did not even bother to ask what movie it was that Freddie referred to.

The plane ride was uneventful. She loved to fly, but not at night when she could not see from the window, and not on a large commercial aircraft which flew too high for her to see anything, except for clouds. She closed her eyes and Freddie read the in-flight magazine, which was about three months out of date. She remembered flying across Mozambique in a small light aircraft. Why was this image in her mind? She could not answer this. But she remembered the tracts of emerald-coloured trees, forests inhabited by people that she would never see or know. Green and more green – trees that grow near the equator are so close to each other that even now, in the comfort of air conditioning and air pressure, she could almost feel the heat and taste the humidity. And the roads that wound through that emerald forest, brown lines flowing through green, structured lines, but ones that created no discernible pattern, a bit like a Cubist painting, linear but not linear enough for her to understand. The city, Beira, the thick air rising up to greet her as the plane taxied gently across the runway. Buildings that came into view, none of them high rises, most of them just houses or tenement buildings where people lived. The Mercedes on the tarmac, racing towards the plane, a war movie. Men in suits with dark glasses covering their eyes, holding guns. It was true, that observation of Freddie's. Guns, no matter who holds them, change a person. She could feel the adrenaline rush through their veins as they stood there – black suits, black sunglasses, guns in the sun. But she was not on her way to Beira now; she was on her way to Johannesburg.

Jan Smuts Airport was full of people, white people. Everywhere she looked she could see white people. It seemed to her she had not seen so many for so long. And they seemed strangely out of place, strangely distasteful. Freddie was collecting their luggage. She gazed around her, bewildered by all the lights and people.

    She stood with her back against the concrete pole. On the top of it was a sign that said *rendezvous*. She supposed that this was where people met each other in this airport. Maybe they knew each other before they met under this pole. Maybe they did not. A woman with yellow hair walked towards her. She wondered if this was a person that she was here to meet, but then she remembered that she was not meeting anyone at this airport. Why would she meet anyone under this concrete pole?

The yellow-haired woman walked up to her. 'Hi,' she said. 'Are you here to give me the parcel that a grandmother has sent to her grandchildren? The parcel with the white rabbits in it.'

'No,' she replied, 'you have the wrong person. I am just standing here waiting, waiting for... my luggage.' I wait and wait and wait, she thought.

'Sorry, wrong person,' the yellow-haired woman said. Her left eyelid jumped a nervous jump. The smoke from her cigarette – one could still smoke in the airport then – curled into the air-conditioner vent that was above them. 'I was just told to meet the person here. It is a parcel for... for my neighbour's child. And of course I don't know what the person from whom I must collect it looks like. And you look like a person who has a present, a surprise maybe?'

'I'm sure that someone will meet you,' she replied. 'How could they possibly forget to deliver a present for a small child?' She saw Freddie and started to walk away. 'Goodbye,' she said to the nameless woman with yellow hair.

Freddie hired a car – a white car, a pure car – and then drove to the hotel where she was to stay.

They checked into the Rosebank Hotel. The lobby moved with the sound of voices, peoples' voices. The walls were painted white and across them hung wine-red pieces of cloth. Victorian England; the light, the white walls and the red drapes. She walked with Freddie across the thick purple carpet. She felt her shoes sink into the lush wool. The lift ride was quick and quiet. The lift was a glass container from which she could see the people below her. They moved like ants. She could not hear them speak. She just followed the movement of their mouths.

In the hotel room, Freddie picked up the heart-shaped chocolate that lay on the pillow of the king-sized bed. 'Maybe you just need a little sugar,' was all Freddie said as she handed her her heart.

Next to the bed on the telephone table was a message written on the hotel stationery. She picked it up and read it. It was from a colleague. 'Let's meet at around eleven in the piano bar downstairs,' was all it said. Freddie looked over her shoulder. 'At least you have some time to get ready,' was her only comment.

She walked into the bathroom and ran the water. At first it was cold and then the hot steam rose upwards towards the ceiling, breath in the cold. In the murky heat she took off her clothes and threw them onto the floor. Then she turned the taps off and climbed into the hot bathtub. On the side of the bath was a packet of bath salts. 'Compliments of the Rosebank Hotel,' were the words on the label. She opened it and poured the salts into the water. An aquamarine seaweed smell mixed with the heat as she lay back and soaked. She tried to wash away the mess of the war, but she could not. As she lay there she wondered where X was. Somewhere in London where it always rains.

X

X walked into the hotel lounge. Maybe it was the hotel bar. Freddie was already sitting at one of the tables. Rick's Café – everyone comes to Rick's, thought Freddie. There were chairs in the bar that were covered in a floral material. Around them were tables. Furniture was scattered around the room. There was a long wooden bar that reached around the back of the wall. Behind the wooden bar were bottles. Tequila, Johnnie Walker, Bols... And between these bottles were photographs of hunters. One stood above a yellow-and-black spotted leopard. Another had his foot on an elephant's trunk, his hand caressing a white ivory tusk. Between them was a lorry filled with lions, and staring above the tangled bodies of the cats were the eyes of a boy. He watched. The eyes were wide. All the animals were dead. Freddie wondered if somewhere in this bar there was an illegal roulette machine. She could hear the ball fall into a magic circle.

    X's black hair was neatly combed and his suit had been dry-cleaned. His white shirt contrasted perfectly with the charcoal jacket. His tie was ironed and touched his waist; just the right length. X stood at the entrance to the room. He looked at his gold watch. He looked around him. He looked at his watch again. Freddie looked at him and said reassuringly, 'Don't worry. They will arrive.' Then she laughed and her tone changed. 'Well,' she said, 'but then maybe they won't.' And she laughed again. What happens if I decide that I don't want them to arrive, she thought. Then what? I suppose X will go home and masturbate... again. I suppose the story will be different. But I think they must arrive, otherwise he will not be here long enough. I must create a pretext for him to stay in this bar.

X looked at his gold watch again. He looked around him again. Then he walked over to a chair and table in the middle of the room and sat down. The room was white except for the waiter and the piano player. Yet, even the waiter wore a white uniform. He had gloves on his hands and a red sash slit his body in half, cutting across his white breast. X called the waiter over. 'A soda please,' he said. The waiter left him alone. I hate these evening meetings, thought X. I hate having to keep my suit on after business hours. And, of course, I will have to eat supper later than I do normally.

He was waiting for two men, two men who would discuss a contract with him. Speaker phones, he thought. I'm here to talk about speaker phones. World-class technology. The waiter brought him his soda water. X paid for it as he looked at his gold watch again. He looked around him again.

Freddie looked up from where she sat and saw them, the two men he was to meet. They saw X and walked over to the table where he sat. I can't write the preliminary greetings, thought Freddie. What the hell do men say when they greet each other? The bonhomie, the absurdity. The pretence of interest. I can't. What the hell will I say?

The two men were dark and sombre, as if they were there to negotiate a contract killing. But on closer scrutiny it was just that they did not smile. They were very, very serious. And they did not have the gangster look. Freddie could not do this. Gangsters are always good looking. Gangsters are romantic. Gangsters wear wrap-around mirrored sunglasses, even at night. And these men had none of these styles. The one man was of average height. He wore a blue open-necked shirt from which chest hair emerged, orange hair that had aged slightly. His lips were thin. The other man was taller than the first man. He wore glasses and had a less-than-average face. Well less than average is still something, thought Freddie. Some are just average; like X.

The men sat down at the table where X sat. The one, with what used to in his youth be orange hair, ordered a Coke, the other something stronger, a whisky and soda. Freddie looked at them and curled up her nose in disdain; it was as if they had a bad odour, the smell of dead octopus. Did they all shake hands? They must have done so, thought Freddie. All men shake hands with each other. Flesh to flesh. Sweat to sweat. A desire to touch the skin of another, another man. And then the men began to talk. And they talked as if the world would end if they did not discuss whatever it was they spoke about. An earnest concerned discussion about the installation of speaker phones.

A weasel-like man sat in the corner of the bar. His facial features were sharp. He was thin. He was dressed smartly. His suit was dark and his tie was covered in red and white stripes. He looked like Peter Lorre, the actor who played the part of the double dealer in the film. He sat alone. He sipped his yellow drink and watched the people around him. I know what he has in his pocket, Freddie thought. I know what he is waiting for. I know that soon that little packet of powder will change hands. And I know that he will walk out of here with more money than a domestic worker makes in a month, maybe even a year. She wondered what he was doing in this room. She sighed as she thought about the weasel man. I wonder why I must make a drug dealer look like a weasel? I suppose that is what people want, she thought. But then why is the image of a weasel shifty and untrustworthy? Prejudice – fear and ignorance, a bigoted view of weasels. And I wonder, are there weasels in Africa or are they European creatures? A weasel – I have never even seen a picture of one before, except for this man, this weasel-like man.

Freddie walked over to the weasel-like man. 'Peter, I have been watching you for a while now,' she said to him, 'and if I did not know differently, if I did not know that this was the first time that you appeared in this story, I would think that you have been doing this all your life.'

'What makes you think I haven't?' the man replied.

'Oh nothing,' Freddie answered, 'but when I first saw you I thought...'

'You thought what?' said the weasel.

Freddie smiled, 'Oh yes, what right do I have to think? I just write words.'

'Shall we make small talk?' the weasel said. 'Is it okay if I just talk to you? I do not want to appear as if I am reluctant to speak to people in this bar. That would make me conspicuous and I do not want that. Too bad about that poor dead girl who was found in the Hillbrow flat after taking too much heroin, isn't it?'

Freddie was bored, but she knew that this was part of the script, so she said, 'I suppose she got a lucky break. Yesterday she was just a lonely unattractive girl. Today she is the honoured dead.'

'You are a very cynical woman,' Peter, the weasel, replied. 'I hope that you will forgive me for saying so. Will you have a drink with me?' He waved at one of the waiters who stood nearby the table. Freddie shook her head. 'Oh, I forgot you never drink with anyone except her, or is it him? Or is it alone?' He turned to the waiter and said, 'Something similar, please. Do you despise me?' He turned back to Freddie.

'If I gave you more words I probably would?' Freddie replied.

'But why? Do you object to the kind of business I do? But think of all those poor people who rely on their powder, who would rot and die if I did not help them. I am not so bad. Through ways of my own I provide them with that which they want so very badly. I provide them with a sort of exit-from-life visa.'

'For a price,' Freddie said. 'For a price.'

'But think of all the poor devils who cannot meet the price that the Nigerians charge. I get it for them for half. Is that so bad? Is that bad in this parasitic world?'

'I don't mind a parasite,' Freddie replied. 'I just don't like a cut-rate one.'

'Well, after tonight, or maybe it will be tomorrow night, I will be through with this whole business and then I am finally leaving this town.' The weasel took an envelope from his pocket and put it on his knee. It lay hidden under the wooden table. 'This is a little of something bigger, more than you will ever see. Good stuff, expensive stuff, stuff of hopes. And tonight, or maybe tomorrow, I will sell it for more money that I have ever dreamed of. And then I am gone, away from this city. Goodbye, Johannesburg. I have not told anyone of this. I wonder why I am telling you. Maybe it is because you despise me that I trust you with this part of my story. I know that you will keep it to yourself. I know that nobody will know what I am about to do. I hope that you are more impressed with me now.'

'I heard a rumour that that poor girl who died in the Hillbrow flat was carrying coke for the Nigerians,' Freddie said. 'And they say that the coke was stolen.'

'I heard that rumour too, poor devil,' replied the weasel. He smiled at Freddie and then he got up and walked away.

The man at the piano played; nostalgic songs from old movies. He was large with a face that smiled. He played as if his heart loved the music. He played as if he had played these songs before. And he *had* played them before, but he had played them a long time ago. Now he played as if he was playing for the last time.

You must remember this, a kiss is just a kiss, a sigh is just a sigh, the fundamental things apply. As time goes by. And when two lovers woo, they both say I love you. On that you can rely, no matter what the future brings, as time goes by.

The black-and-white piano keys moved in time to the music. A grey shadow hovered over the piano. It moved together with the hands of the piano player.

At a table nearby sat seven people. Freddie looked at them and wondered what the best words would be to describe them. I can't say fascist, for what does a fascist look like? Hitler was swarthy and he had a thin black moustache just above his top lip, a cockroach sitting on his mouth. The blonde and beautiful young German schoolboys who sang about the *Übermensch* in the movie *Cabaret* were young. They were so innocent. The Spanish fascists did not look as modern and spotless as Ronald Reagan did; their shirts were stained with the red mountain dust. And none of them looked like Margaret Thatcher or held a handbag. Well, I suppose, once again, it is a particularly South African stereotype; fascist clothing, khaki pants and khaki shirts, apartheid clothing in a bar. You know what I mean. It is the way they comb their hair. It is slicked down with oil. And I suppose it is their size. They are fat. Why is it that the description of a fascist is always of an overweight fascist? I mean, Thatcher was thin, so was PW Botha. Oh fuck, I can't seem to write anything that is not a cliché, Freddie mused. Fat; I suppose it is the amount of food you must eat to be a fascist, otherwise how could you be one? And, after all, you will always have enough food in this kind of world. Fascists are well fed and comfortable, or otherwise they can afford to diet. And nowadays the word 'fat' is so derogatory. And these men made loud noises. They belched often. They drank beer. They were drunk. Well, maybe they sort of do look a bit like Margaret Thatcher, just a fatter version. Although they do not speak English with a posh ersatz accent or wear a designer suit that may have been bought at Marks & Spencer. They wore khaki.

Freddie looked at X. He was deep in discussion. He was talking about something very, very serious. In fact all of the men with him were very serious. They stroked their cocks as they spoke. Was this a reflex action? When you talk about important things do you, without thinking about it, stroke your cock? Or is this deliberate, thought Freddie? Do they all want to feel their manliness? Their important manly conversation.

A man with a Nikon camera around his neck walked into the room and sat down. The camera had a long lens attached to it. He was a photojournalist. He looked at objects and people and immobilised them in motionless pictures. He was a visitor in the reality of others. And when he had seen all that he wanted to see he just moved on to another photograph, the adjectives of others. Soon a woman joined him. They asked for drinks. It was ten thirty at night. The table of fascists all looked at the man with the camera as he sat down. One of them pointed at him. He, or was it Margaret Thatcher, said something inaudible and then he got up and walked over to the cameraman. 'What the fuck are you doing with that in here?' he said loudly, so that everyone who sat in the room could hear him. 'What the fuck do you want to do with that?' He pointed at the camera. 'Okay, take my picture. Take it.' He pulled his shirt open. Underneath his shirt, resting on his matted chest hair, or was it on his breasts, was a crucifix and a swastika. Jesus, on his gold cross, looked bemused as he writhed in pain. Freddie thought she heard an unhappy donkey bray.

The photojournalist stood up, and then he sat down again. 'It's for my work. I've just come in from a job, but now work is over for today.' His tone was jaded. He had heard this before. He had seen this before. 'Although,' and he leaned forward towards the drunken man or woman who wore the crucifix and the swastika, 'although, if you wore a fedora it would make a great picture. You, I mean, you would look great in a picture.'

Freddie laughed. I wonder what I find attractive, she thought as she listened to the exchange. Can you picture these men or women? Can you see the photograph? Do you know what X looks like? Do you know what my sometimes-different-gender protagonist looks like? And if I describe them to you, would they look as if they could be in a magazine or in a movie? Will they be interesting looking or just plain? If I describe a Hollywood movie star to you would you even recognise the person that I describe; Humphrey Bogart or, maybe, Ingrid Bergman? What would they look like if they were beautiful, my characters? I wonder.

'Yes, you look great, so great,' the photojournalist continued. 'Love your jewellery.' He reached out to touch the crucifix and the swastika. The drunken fascist moved backwards. He did not want to be touched by another man. People might think he was queer. In fact, he did not want to be touched. He ordered women to touch him. They did not do so gratuitously. And Margaret Thatcher never touched anyone. He looked at the man with the camera, and he could not respond. After all, what could he say? What could Freddie say? So he moved away, back to his own table. Back to his ubiquitous alcohol.

He walked into the bar and looked for them – the two of them, the man with the camera and the woman who was with him. 'Remember,' said Freddie, 'he is a journalist too.' Freddie pointed them out to him, for by now the bar had filled up and it was difficult to make out the different faces in the dim of the night light. 'Wait a minute before you go up to them,' Freddie said to him. 'The conversation with the drenched and drunken fascist is still going on. I will finish it now, so just wait.' And so, he waited.

As he did so he looked around him. In the half-light of the bar he saw the piano man, black fingers on white keys. Play my song, he said to himself. Play it again, Sam.

'No,' said Freddie softly, 'it is *Play it Sam. Play it Sam.*' It was Woody Allen who changed the phrase; Woody Allen put the word 'again' into it.

He continued to look at the man at the piano; it was if he had seen him somewhere before. It was as if this scene had been played somewhere before. *Déjà vu*, he thought.

'No,' said Freddie, '*Casablanca*. In fact, there are several scenes with the piano man, or as Ilsa says, "*the boy who plays the piano*". And he plays the same song. The same song, over and over again.'

The drunken man finished his beer with the black label on it and left the table. He looked at himself sideways in the mirror above the bar, and through the corner of his eye he thought he looked good. He thought he might just look like Margaret Thatcher. His khaki trousers bulged.

And what does my character, the hero, look like? Freddie thought. I think I must put something in here, just to fill out this passage, just so that you think that you know him a little better. Just so you have an image of him. Well he is a bit like that boy, or is he a girl, from the Calvin Klein underwear advertisement that hangs on the billboard in Time Square. But he has clothes on. Does this short description bring a picture of him to your mind? Or will it only bring a picture of him to the minds of those who have been to Time Square? Those who have been able to see the billboard. Or even those who know about Calvin Klein and read fashion magazines. A selective description, a description that condemns those who do not know this advertisement to knowing nothing. He is the original capitalist illusion, in the same way that everyone else is, different and unique. He has his own perfect space in the world that nobody else can penetrate. He lives on a billboard in Time Square. And yet my character is insecure about what his physical appearance shows you. Strange how the Calvin Klein boy earns millions of dollars and my character is insecure about what he appears to be to a world where only a few can see him. There, I have told you what he looks like. I have written these words and yet I do not think you really know what he looks like. I have not described him to you at all. But what are his thoughts? I do not know. Everyone has a thought as to what they look like and so when I describe him, maybe he is nothing like this at all. And my words, what do they mean when I look at him? Nothing. Just something to me and to someone who has been to Time Square in New York City.

And then the Calvin Klein boy looked into the mirror. X was reflected in it. X next to a Calvin Klein boy – a billboard in a Johannesburg hotel mirror. 'Take that shocked look off your face,' said Freddie. 'It is a mirror image of him. Or maybe it even *is* him. Do nothing. Go and join your friends.' At the same time X also looked up. Their eyes met in the reflection. Then he walked over to the table where the photojournalist and the woman sat. The camera was on the table.

'Hi,' he said.

The man and the woman looked up. 'Hi. Wow, it's great to see you,' said the woman.

The man with the camera looked at him and smiled.

'Welcome to the big city,' he said, and leaned over his drink. Then he kissed him on the lips. 'Welcome. Good to see you in this hellhole. How is Mozambique? You've been putting in some great stuff. What are you in love with?'

'I love the decay of the city, the burlesque of the West,' he replied, and then he laughed. His hands shook and his lips glowed. He sat down.

'Why are you shaking?' the photojournalist said. 'Can't be that you're in a whites-only bar. You've been into one before. Thought we could meet you here and then move on. Hate this sort of bourgeois bullshit myself. Look at them.' He pointed at X and his colleagues. X and his sober colleagues. 'Look at those fucks in their suits. What are they? Just fucking suits. Where is the person? And look at those ones.' He looked at the table of fascists. He did not point to them. 'Jesus Christ, I prefer the Harare beat myself.'

He looked at the table that the photojournalist pointed to. He looked at X. He stared at X. And X looked back at him. Then X moved his lips into a smile. He was not sure why he did this. He just curled up the corners of his lips. Maybe one of his colleagues had made a joke. X turned to the man with the grey-orange hair and said something important.

The cameraman called to a waiter. 'What do you want?' he said. 'I'll have another whisky.'

'I'll have one too,' he said, as he took out a packet of Mozambican cigarettes; *Liberté* – the words were written on the box. He continued to stare at X.

'Go on. Keep on staring,' said Freddie. 'Maybe if you stare so hard he will just disappear. He could be an illusion. But stop shaking. Look at your hands – the way that cigarette moves. It is not windy in here. How terrifying is he, this X of yours? He is pretty in a bland sort of way, but that's it – not much else to him. I know. I have seen him and, although you don't know this, I have already written about what he does when he goes to a Johannesburg supermarket. Not much, I can tell you. He just ticks off things on a list.'

The brown shirts at the table nearby were getting noisy.

The man – or was it Margaret Thatcher? – with the swastika and the cross around his neck thumped the table with his empty bottle. 'More... More! I want another one,' he shouted. 'Where is the service in this place? Can't you employ some whites here? These *kaffirs* are useless.' He grinned and shouted at the waiter who walked over to the table. 'Move, you *hout kop*,' he said. The waiter did not move any faster. He picked up the empty bottle from the table and wiped it clean of the spilled alcohol.

The waiter brought a glass of whisky to his table.

He took a long gulp of the yellow liquid. It tasted beautiful, harsh and hot. 'Look, look over there,' said Freddie. 'I wish there was a balcony here, then we could watch the scene from above, as Rick did. A picture from above always makes the watcher more powerful, superior to those whom you watch.'

A khaki shirt stood up. He gestured to his comrades around the table to do the same. They too stood. And then he started to sing. As he sang he banged on the table with his glass bottle. The liquid jolted in the container. It flew out of it and into the air. Then it landed on the polished wood.

'Uit die blou van onse hemel, uit die diepte van ons see. Oor ons ewige gebergtes, waar die kranse antwoord gee...'

X looked up. He looked up. Freddie looked up. The brown of the shirts fixed itself against the bodies of the fascists. Their faces were covered in salty sweat. He got up. His face was flushed pink. He hesitated. 'Yes,' said Freddie, 'you can do it. It is in the script. It is fine. And after all, what is nationalism? Just another inane and stupid emotion, but at least it is an emotion. So you have love and you have a bit of national spirit. Absurd, but you have it anyway.'

He walked over to the piano player. The piano player looked at him. Then his Calvin Klein face bent forward. He whispered something into the piano player's ear. Then he walked back to the table. 'I feel as if I have done a great thing,' he said to Freddie as he walked. 'I have just done a great thing. I have become a hero.'

'No,' Freddie thought, 'no, I just allow you to blow with the wind. And, at the moment, this is the prevailing wind, the wind by which we measure what is right. Well, we all know where it all will end, so I must make you take the side that will win. You are, after all, the protagonist of this story. But you can feel as if you have done a great and laudable thing.'

No one noticed him; no one saw him whispering to the man who played the piano. The piano player's black face smiled. As his mouth opened his teeth emerged, pearls from an oyster. He played a note. '*Nkosi sikelel' iAfrika,*' he began. His voice was soft. Then his voice became high and shaky. '*Nkosi sikelel' iAfrika. Maluphakanyisw...*' The piano notes joined in with his voice. The keys became louder. A waiter with a bottle of champagne on a tray stopped walking towards the table that he was serving. He put the tray down. He raised his right hand into the air. His hand moved into a fist. The barman stopped shaking the martini shaker. He put the olive that he had picked up into his mouth. He chewed and swallowed. Then he to raised his right arm. With his left hand, for the other was now raised, he removed the olive pip from his mouth and threw it across the bar. Then another waiter stopped what he was doing. Then another... Then another... Then another. In the doorway to the bar the doorman in his red-and-white slave uniform and the receptionist with braided hair gathered. The photojournalist stood up. He too raised his right arm. The woman at his table did so too. Soon there were more people standing in the bar.

Where have they come from, he wondered as a tear filled his eye.

'You see,' said Freddie, 'nothing matters anymore. You can do anything in a movie.' And they sang.

'*Nkosi sikelel' iAfrika. Maluphakanyisw' uphondo lwayo, Yizwa imithandazo yethu, Nkosi sikelela, thina lusapho lwayo. Morena boloka setjhaba sa heso, O fedise dintwa la matshwenyeho, O se boloke, O se boloke setjhaba sa heso, Setjhaba sa South Afrika – South Afrika...*'

END

A gilded whore at the bar picked up her gin, and then she put it down again. She did not know the words to the song, but a small tear fell from her painted eye and made the mascara run black down her face. It united with her white face powder and became beige, almost brown, as it moved downwards. She stood up and cried.

Even Freddie felt a tear in her eye. She wondered why. And then she thought, this scene always makes me cry. It is okay I suppose. I wonder why I am crying, but then who really cares with emotion? It does not matter what it is that evokes the emotion. So if I can cry, maybe you can too. And a tear moved down Freddie's cheek. And as she cried, she wondered if this scene was as moving as the one in which Laszlo did the same thing. It was *La Marseillaise* then, now it is *God Bless Africa*. And she always cried when that scene showed in the movie.

X looked up. He stood up, but it was only for a moment. Then he sat down again. He is embarrassed, Freddie thought. Well if he can't stand, he is a coward.

X's colleague, who had his glasses hooked over his nose, turned to X, and then to the other man who had the orange hair. He said something to them. He pulled his wallet from his jacket pocket and threw some money onto the table. Freddie looked at them. He looked at them. But he could not hear what any of them said. Then he looked at X and smiled, a hero's smile. X and his colleagues then got up and walked out of the bar. He continued to look at X as his smile faded. Then cold hell broke loose. And there was no exit.

Just what we like to think of as hell, Freddie thought. The waiters stopped singing and moved to the sides of the room. They pushed against its walls. The barman picked up another olive and put it in his mouth. The piano man continued to play, but he had changed the tune.

'*You must remember this, a kiss is just a kiss, a sigh is just a sigh. The fundamental things apply. As time goes by...*'
The khaki shirts looked vicious. There was stillness except for the notes of the piano.

'And when two lovers woo, they both say I love you. On that you can rely, no matter what the future brings, as time goes by...'

Two policemen accompanied by the hotel manager ran into the bar. A blue hand snatched at a waiter's neck. A khaki shirt punched another waiter in the face, then kicked the white uniform with the red sash onto the floor. The photojournalist picked up his camera. Click click click. Motionless history for his newspaper's readers.

A blue policeman walked over to the piano man and pushed his hands roughly from the keys. 'Stop playing!' he screamed. 'Stop playing!' He grabbed the microphone that the piano man used and shouted. 'Closed!' he shouted. 'All out! Everyone out, except for the blacks. And you can stay.' He addressed the khaki shirts. 'Stay and help us with this mess.' The piano man moved away from the piano. He carefully closed the lid and covered the black-and-white keys.

Peter, the weasel, sat alone and watched. Freddie watched him as he watched. Then she saw him stand up. He was a ghost among people; no one noticed what he did. His hand felt in his jacket pocket. It touched something. He looked around him again. Then he walked nonchalantly over to the piano and slipped something into the open top, next to where one piece of wood joined another, the joint that raised the lid. He blended quietly with the chaos around him. Then he slithered to the entrance of the bar and walked away.

Freddie walked with him as he started to leave the bar. He still held his whisky glass. 'Drink it,' said Freddie. 'Why waste it? We can get another in the room later.' He gulped down the yellow liquid.

The cameraman walked towards him. 'I've got the shots I need and she will write it up. Great place to come for a drink.' The cameraman winked, 'Sleep well, my darling.' He turned and left the bar.

'Come,' said Freddie, 'let's go.' She took his arm. They walked to the lifts. The lift arrived and they climbed into it. On the third floor they walked out of the lift doors and went to room number 356. The door closed behind them with a soft thud.

He sat on the bed. The shock of seeing X in the bar smothered him. He could not breathe. His heart raced. He must see him. He must find him again. The scene in the bar rose up in front of his eyes. X silhouetted against the blur of bodies. X in the window of the camera. X who had walked away from him.

Freddie realised that he was in a grim mood. 'Come,' she said. 'Go to bed.'

'No,' he replied.

'Are you ever going to bed?' Freddie asked.

'No, I am not sleepy,' he replied.

'Well then, how about a drink?' Freddie continued.

'No, Freddie,' he said, 'I am waiting for a lady, or maybe I am waiting for a man – how would I know? Maybe I should just get out of here. There seems to be nothing but trouble in this city.'

'He is coming back,' Freddie said. 'I know that X will come back. How can he not do so now that he has seen you?'

'Maybe we can take a car, maybe we can just drive all night, maybe we can get drunk or go fishing. I need you tonight, Freddie. I need you to shut up, but don't leave me alone. Not tonight, don't leave me tonight.'

'I will stay here all night,' said Freddie. 'Maybe I should start playing the piano – then I could be more like Sam. I could play the piano and comfort you. You and I have to remain together. Until after the story is complete that is.'

'If it is December in Johannesburg,' he spoke softly, 'what time is it in Maputo? I bet that they are asleep in Maputo. Marina is asleep. Her mother is asleep, even though it is always as if she has closed her eyes. Regina is asleep. Amir is asleep. The nurse with the ruby in her nose is asleep. I bet they're asleep all over Mozambique now. Of all the gin joints in the world, why did I have to walk into this one? Play me that song that the piano man played in the bar, Freddie. Play it to me. I will find out if I can still stand it.'

'I don't remember it,' Freddie said, 'and I cannot play the piano.'

He stared ahead, out of the window, but could see nothing except the lights from the street. He stared at Freddie and then he put his head between his hands.

You must remember this. A kiss is just a kiss, a sigh is just a sigh. It's still the same old story, the fight for love and glory, a case of do or die… the fundamental things of life… No matter what the future brings. As time goes by.

XI

X climbed into his off-white Toyota Corolla. There was mud on the side of it; he must have driven through a puddle of water on the way to the hotel. His moist hands shook. 'It is not the bar-room brawl that makes you shake,' said Freddie. 'It is that you saw her. You saw her in a place where you least expected to. You do not even know what the song is about. It means nothing to you. It is a foreign language. The emotion that filled the voices of the waiters meant nothing. But you saw her, the reflection in the mirror, and you were afraid.'

X said nothing. He could neither agree, nor could he disagree. Then he turned the ignition key. The car started, but he could not move his hand to put it into first gear. He turned the ignition off. The car park was silent, except for the coughing of the security guard who prowled aimlessly next to the boom that blocked the path to the street. X opened the door of the car and got out.

'That's right,' Freddie said, 'do it. The script says that you have to do it and how can I change what it is you have to do?' X walked towards the entrance of the hotel. He looked at his watch. It was late, but he knew that Y would not be home. She was probably in another part of the city; a street where only the mad or the desperate went at night. Or in the day for that matter, thought Freddie. X knew that he did not need to hurry.

He walked up to the reception and mumbled something to the person behind the desk.

'It's 356, Sir,' said the receptionist. A tired-looking woman with dyed blonde hair had replaced the black woman whose head was covered in braids. 'Do you want me to call and say that you are on your way up?'

'No,' X replied, 'I am expected.' He did not wink at the dyed blonde hair. She was confused. He should have winked. This is what those who were in the hotel for a sexual tryst did. X turned and walked to the lifts. The doors opened and he moved inside – into the glass bowl. He moved upwards.

The bed was in the centre of the room. On the right was a chintz-covered chair that was supposed to be comfortable. Freddie sat in it. It is a reading chair, thought Freddie, or otherwise I suppose it could be moved so that a person could watch the television. A book, a television soap opera, much the same thing, Freddie thought. She leaned backwards and watched the scene before her. She would not speak now, she decided. Now was not the time to say anything. Just let the pictures, or maybe the words, show themselves. Next to the wall, opposite the bed, was a table. I wish that you were not so drunk, thought Freddie. If you were not so drunk you would not have this gushing of emotion. It is gushing down like the fucking Victoria Falls. Emotions are such a waste of time, especially emotion for X. Well not just for X, for anything. Freddie continued to think alone. Emotions never seem to take anyone anywhere. I wonder why people have them. All they do is sustain an illusion. More emotion, more illusion, more illusion, more emotion, more illusion, and so it goes on. Useless.

Freddie watched her as she picked up the bottle and poured herself another whisky. The bottle slipped from her hand – a crash – and the liquid wickedly covered the table and dripped to the floor. But she did not notice it. Freddie looked at her face. There were no tearstains on it. Her eyes were dead, her mouth hard, with lips that were straight and metallic – a knife. Her mouth moved mechanically as she opened it to take another sip from the whisky glass. Then the door made a sound. Freddie looked up; she was expecting this sound. She knew who stood behind the wooden barrier. At the same time she looked towards the window, for the sound echoed around the room and was now floating about near the double-glazed, security-barred glass.

'Where is that sound coming from?' she said to Freddie with an irritable twang to her voice. 'Does this hotel have rats in it? Must remind myself to tell them to put out the rat killer... Rat killer that is what is needed here if I am going to get any sleep.' Her brow wrinkled as she remembered what her mother had told her when she was a child. 'Rat killer kills rats. It is effective because they like to eat it. It tastes like sugar. But then once they have eaten even a small tiny bit of that powder they are filled with an overwhelming thirst. They feel tired and are overcome with lassitude. They try to get to water, but they cannot move, as they are so tired. And then these rodents, these filthy rodents swell up and dehydrate. Within hours, if you look you will find them dead – all puffed up with and their tongues hanging out.'

That is a great image, thought Freddie. Dead rats with tongues hanging from their mouths. What happens when the bodies rot? I wonder if they smell. The smell of death. Lifelessness. Do maggots fall from their loose dead flesh? The dream of Scylla, her love lost along with her face, staring out from the straits of the sea. And yet Scylla did not think about smell.

Freddie turned to where she sat and said to her, 'No, I don't think it is rats. I don't think that they are going to die in this room.' She took another sip from the glass. The whisky ran down her chin and dripped onto her black Levi jeans. 'But I do think it's rats,' she replied. 'What else would make that sound? Or maybe I am just waiting for a lady, or is it a man? I can't be sure. It's been such a long while since I saw the movie. It is the sound of a lady. Did I say that before? Whisky makes me repeat myself.' She got up and walked towards the telephone. Her hand touched the receiver.

Freddie stopped her. 'Listen again,' she said.

The sound came. It was louder now. She looked at the door and laughed, 'Well I could open it and let the rats come running in.

Then you'll see that I was right all along.'

'Maybe X makes that sort of sound,' Freddie said.

She walked to the door and opened it. X stood there. She moved towards him, mumbling, 'Where are the rats. You have to stop them from coming in here. They bite, you know. They bite the dead.'

X lingered for a moment outside the door before walking into the room. He wrinkled his nose. He smelt the strong smell of the spilt whisky – the fragrance of loveliness. He looked at her. There was no expression on her face. It was impassive, blank, opaque.

'If you want a whisky there's more in the cupboard, or in the mini bar. Maybe there's even some chocolate in there – if you want chocolate to line your stomach. That's all that I have here. White chocolate for strength.' She laughed. 'I saved my first drink to have with you.'

'No, not tonight. I can't drink now it's so late,' said X.

She reached out for the whisky bottle but could not find it. It was in shards. Freddie handed another to her. 'I thought you lived in London,' she said. 'I thought you never came to Johannesburg. I thought that if you were going to come here at least you would have sent me a letter so that we could meet. So why are you here? There are other places.'

Freddie looked at her. If I have to have some emotion here, she thought, surely it can only be sympathy. How does a person respond when love walks into the room? Pity – is that what I feel? Pity is such a feeble emotion. It degrades the person that you pity. What can I write so that pity is not the pervasive feeling? What can I write so that the reader does not pity her?

'Well, if you won't have a drink, then I will,' she said to X. 'Have one. Don't think that it's poisoned. Why would I want to poison you?' And she laughed as she thought about the rats and their dehydrated bloated bodies. X with a dehydrated and bloated body.

'I would not have come to this hotel if I had known that you were here. I didn't know that you would be here,' X said. 'Believe me, it's true.'

'It's funny, your voice hasn't changed,' she said. 'I can still hear it. "If I could, I would go with you any place. We'll get on a train together and never stop." Why are you here?' She spoke to him as if he were not in the room. X looked at her, then she looked at Freddie. 'What must I say?' she asked Freddie. Her voice was pleading and desperate.

Freddie said nothing. Why should she say anything, she thought. Why put words into her mouth?

'I understand how you feel,' said X.

'You understand how I feel,' she said. Her voice had risen slightly, but only Freddie noticed this. 'You understand how I feel. How long was it that we had? I remember the days, every fucking last one of them. The sand and the sea and the storm and me sitting waiting for a letter with a comical look on my face because my insides had been kicked out. And I counted the more and more and more days that I waited for a letter with the head of the queen pasted in the right hand corner of the envelope.'

Freddie prompted her now. 'Oh yes, when was it – the last time we met? All those moving bodies in the bar reminded me of the Casa do Sol. And a fight... hey.' The glass moved to her mouth.

'I came up because I couldn't just walk away,' X said.

'Big boy,' said Freddie. 'What a big boy you are.'

'Let me tell you a story. It's a long one,' X continued.

She interrupted him. 'Has it got a wow finish?'

'And you couldn't even tell the truth at the beginning,' Freddie continued. 'I wonder what it is that has given you this big size. Is it because you are in your own town now? Does that give you a sense of ownership, of comfort? You're in your own war now.'

'I didn't know that you'd be coming to Johannesburg and least of all that we would bump into each other in this hotel. There are thousands of hotels in this town,' X continued.

'Yes, I wonder now why you stepped into this gin joint,' she said.

'I live here,' X said. 'I live here with someone who once

made me believe that the world was wonderful and beautiful. And I was filled with the ideals and knowledge that she gave to me. I thought that I worshipped her. This girl was beautiful, this girl was brave, and this girl looked at life as if it did not have a tomorrow. And I stayed with this girl. I stayed with her because she inspired me. She made me think that maybe there would be no tomorrow and that there was always today. She made me live. Now that girl lives life differently. Now that girl still believes that there is only today, but today is a little bit different as to how it looked yesterday. And that girl needs me. I suppose I was in love. I am still in love with that memory. I suppose I am nostalgic for a past and so I stay. But now...'

'Yes,' she said. 'I've heard this kind of story before. As a matter of fact, I've heard a lot of stories in my life. It is my job, you know, to listen to stories. They all begin with, "Mister, I once met a girl." Who is this girl? Did you go back to her or were there others in between? Or aren't you the kind that tells?' She looked at him. The expression on her face had changed from one of impassivity to one of anger.

Freddie looked at them. 'Don't be angry,' Freddie whispered to her. 'Don't be angry. If you are angry it means that you care. I am never angry because I don't care enough, and anger changes nothing. Although now you are making me care about you, so I had better start a different story. And anyway you are meant to look resigned – that's what Bogart was, resigned and drunk.'

'So why did you come back?' she asked X. 'Your voice,' she continued, and this time she faced X, 'your voice hasn't changed. I remember you saying, "Darling, I will write, we will talk. Maybe some day you will visit me in London and we can walk down to Piccadilly Circus. Maybe someday we can be together again and this time for longer, lots longer... lots longer." Tell me why you really ran out on me.'

X stared at her. 'I've told you, there is nothing else that I can say,' he said.

'Why not? I want to hear everything. After all I'm the one stuck with a false memory.'

X did not want her to stop speaking. He wanted her voice. Her voice turned him on. Her sarcasm bit into his veins. His blood moved in haste. She did not raise her voice, but the sound was loud. She spoke with a quiet dignity. The voice was dignified. What X remembered of her was not. He remembered her on her knees. He remembered her fingers. He remembered how she would touch herself, her whole hand almost inside her cunt. She begged for more of him and he would smile.

'Do I look comical to you now as I say these things? I feel comical. I feel like a clown. Clowns are always sad; clowns are always having their insides kicked out. I was happy, so happy. Well, happiness is a pretty clownish condition, isn't it? Stop now with the smiles and the sniggers. Don't applaud me my sentiment.'

X sat down on the bed. Freddie stared at him. What could X say now? He could give no apology, for that surely would be trite. He could give no excuse, or could he?

'I do want a whisky,' X said at last.

'Pour one yourself,' she replied. 'I don't want to move from here. I have a ringside view of you, and I want to see you when you speak and drink.' She put her finger in her mouth. 'Let us change sides now.' She looked at him with what may have been humour.

Freddie got up and put the radio on. She needed music in this room – music to dim the lights, music to keep the passionate momentum. She moved the dial of the radio so that the rap music changed to opera, the death of Tosca.

She got up and went to X. Freddie sat and watched her. While she watched she played with the dials on the radio.

'Listen to the music. Does it sound like a tinny piano to you? Well, it should because I've heard a lot of stories that start in the same way that yours does.' She walked over to where X was sitting, almost stepping on Freddie's outstretched foot as she stumbled. Then she bent over and kissed X on the mouth. Her red lipstick left a bloodstain where their lips met. X got up. He opened the door and walked out.

Bright red, red, like the sky at night, red like the ruby the Indian nurse wore in her nose, red, red... Red for the dead child, the child in death, but he had already been born.

Well, thought Freddie, maybe that was over doing it. But what else could I do? I like those lines and they fit into the story.

XII

He needed something outside the closed space of the hotel room. The room was airless; it smelt of spilt whisky and spilt sex. The red stain on X's lips haunted him. He felt as if he was bleeding. The stain was on the bed, it was on his shirt, it covered his hands and when he looked into the mirror, which was on top of the dressing table, the stain moved around his face. It travelled down his forehead and then touched his nose. It sat near to the corner of his eye. Then it lingered hauntingly on his lip-stained mouth and moved on downwards. And the whisky lay on the table, transparent on the wood. It too would leave a stain. There was no wind and the table was so flat that it could not move with gravity. It was still, a grid. A golden net that covered him.

'I need to get out of here for a few minutes,' he said to Freddie.

'It is late and I am tired,' Freddie replied, 'but I may as well come with you, even though I need to get some sleep. Let's go for a walk.'

'I think that's what I need,' he said, and as he said it he thought how good it would be to be alone, outside the people in his life, just in the words.

He opened the door of the room and walked into the passage. It was silent. The hotel was asleep. He pressed the button to call the lift. It came upwards quickly. The doors opened and he walked inside. The lift moved to the ground floor. He walked past Rick's Café and as he did so he looked into it. The glass doors were closed. It was littered with the debris of the evening's fracas. A table lay on its side, its legs facing east.

A chair stood on three legs, one of them broken off. Maybe it had been used as a cudgel. Maybe the thin wooden pieces were now splinters in a person's head. A lone worker in a short pink and white maid's uniform knelt in front of a policeman. The policeman had stayed behind in the café to ensure that all that remained in this room stayed in revolt. The young woman raised her eyes from the policeman's groin as he walked passed the café. Her dark thick pink lips covered a pale hairless cock. She worked her red tongue around the swollen glands so that when she sucked this raised high human object would receive the most pleasure. And she was on her knees; it was if she was begging him for something more. But she was not; she was a vampire sucking at his life. The policeman's face was contorted into a grimace of wonder, a grimace of guilt, a grimace of hope. She stayed on her knees as his semen spurted from the needle hole at the end of his cock. The policeman gave a sigh, then leaned back into the chair and closed his eyes. The young woman stayed on her knees. She turned her head and spat the semen from her mouth. Her tongue licked her teeth. Then she wiped the floor of the yellow custard-like liquid and collected the shards of glass that lay next to it.

'An interesting display, isn't it.' He heard the voice of a yellow-haired woman next to him. She stood upright. 'And all I wanted to do was go in there and have a drink. It is not that late and this bar always stays open until the early hours of the morning. Everybody knows this, which is why the night people always come here. Just a quick drink, I thought, before I have to deliver something. The arrangement is for later, and I am early for my delivery.'

He looked towards the voice. It was familiar. It was low and breathless. The yellow hair was the same yellow hair that had stood under the *rendezvous* sign in the airport. The parcel from a grandmother to her grandchild was in her right hand. It was a small package. He wondered what a grandmother would send to a child that could be so small. Maybe a piece of jewellery. A golden cross with Jesus writhing on it. Maybe a St Christopher for a safe journey. 'I was just going out for a walk when I also thought of getting a drink,' he said. He knew that this was untrue; he had really just wanted to go inside the bar and find the glass that X had held. He wanted to put it to his lips and drink from it. He wanted to bite the glass so that fragments of it splintered into his tongue and broke the skin. He wanted to mix his blood with X's saliva. He wanted to bleed some more.

'Well, let's walk then anyway,' the yellow woman replied. 'I have to deliver this just now and not here in this bar, so I will have to leave here anyway. Oh, the person did arrive at the airport to give it to me. You were right. How could a grandmother forget her grandchild?' She laughed. 'And we can walk in the direction that I have to go in. There are cabs down that side, and it's a nice walk, under the purple arches of jacaranda. Maybe we can even sit down for a bit in an open space, which by day is a café. By night it is chairs with just a lone waiter waiting for someone, waiting for something. And then we can smoke. I'm Y, by the way.'

He followed her down the stairs that led to the outside. Together they walked down the road. Pools of light from the streetlamps lit up the pavement, bright circles of yellow on the grey asphalt. As he walked outside the pool it became dark again. He jumped from pool to pool. When he was inside one he felt that she was looking at him, even though he knew that she had her head faced forward and she did not let her eyes wander towards him. But in the light he was in a spotlight, on a stage, a set for a movie. He did not know which movie it was. She was silent. So was he.

They moved towards the tables. It was a silent place, there was no one there except, as Y had said, a lone waiter. The waiter looked at them. He knew that they would not require too much attention. He could continue with his fantasy. He walked over to the table.

'Whisky for me,' Y said to the waiter, and, for the first time since they had begun to walk, she turned to him. 'And you?'

'Oh... me too,' he said.

The waiter removed himself from their space and walked

through the slim door of the café.

'I wonder what you are doing on this street tonight,' Y asked. 'I sort of know what I am doing. I am being the kind deliverer of a package to a poor loved grandchild. Not sure why I am doing this. I don't really like children.' A piece of her hair blew into the corner of her mouth and she put out her tongue to take it into the dark red cavern. 'Everyone seems to have children, and if they don't then they have a cat. I suppose it is a biological imperative that all women need to bear children so that the race will continue. Biology disguised as good sex. Or maybe disguised as selfless sharing. No one else will need you to share your life with them. Or is it just plain fear that makes people reproduce, the fear of death, the need for immortality, immortality through your own genes? The need not to be alone. Maybe it is just ego, the need to be so desperately needed. I wonder. And I suppose all a cat won't give one in this equation is good sex. Sex maybe, but how good can it be with a cat? Ugh, all that hair... especially if it is one of those Persian sorts.'

Freddie walked towards them. He looked up. Maybe she just wanted to listen to this conversation, as she was writing it down. It was a bit one-edged. Y spoke, he did not. He was reminded of the times that he had listened, without speaking, to X. Maybe it was because he did not carry a package for anyone's children. How could he know. Freddie sat down. Y appeared not to notice her. She continued as if it were just the two of them who sat there. 'Just talk,' Freddie said. 'Don't mind me.' Y did not mind Freddie sitting there. She had not even noticed that they were no longer alone.

'Children are like drugs or alcohol,' Y continued. 'An addiction, a childish addiction. Mmmm... This chosen addiction, like drugs and alcohol.' She seemed to be talking to herself. 'Children fasten people into the pointlessness of existence. Drugs offer a way out of living because then you can live in a world that is false and untrue. You create it, you die in it, and you can pretend. Maybe, well that's what I think. Not sure why I think this though.'

'It does not matter if you know why you think this,' Freddie said. 'Why should it? If you think that drugs point to a way out, even thought the rest of the world frowns on the way out because they only feel secure in the world if they believe everyone is really there in it with them, everyone is as grey and sober as themselves. You think they give you a way out as they change the world for you. They alter the way that you see things. They expand your mind. Would they do the same for X? I sort of think that they wouldn't. He can't expand, or at least I don't think that he can. Maybe you know him better than I do.'

'Not sure if I know him better than you do,' Y said. 'I think I only know the one part of him, the suburban home part. Does he have a tragic movie hero side?'

Freddie did not answer the question. Instead she said, 'Of course, drugs damage as well, but that is the price you pay for trying to get out of this place. You may as well die living.'

'I wish I were a man,' he suddenly said to Y.

'You are a man, at least for a while, in this chapter,' Freddie said to him, but as he did not hear her he just continued to talk. 'Women are constantly preoccupied with the marginal things in life. Love and children and no violence, they are important only in that if they were not there, there would be no world for us, but that is all.'

'Important things,' Y said, 'more important... much more important. What is more important than immortality? What does it mean? We always think that what we are doing is not as important as what someone else is doing. But nothing is important at all. Not children, not your work... What is it that you do?'

'I think that I did not express myself correctly,' he continued. 'Not that what we do, or what anyone does is important, but that it is so much easier to be a man in the world. Take X for instance, he never gets stuck in the world of sentiment. He just says that he loves whoever his wife is and then he moves on to something else. And I just sit and think about how negligible my love for him is. The more interesting things belong to a man's world. Women are forced to ramble on about love and sentiment and the runny noses of their children and all of that bullshit in order to try rationalise their existence. I am confused, maybe men do that too, only the subject matter is different. But the subject matter is so much easier and more comfortable.'

'The subject matter is different,' Freddie said. 'But it is the same sort of thing.'

'I wish I were a man,' Y interjected, 'because it is easier to be a man. Safer – others think that men are stronger than women so they defer to this strength, whatever it is, strength of their muscles, strength of their brains. And so they can have a lot more fun than women do. I have a husband,' she laughed. 'Yes I do. I know that it is not so believable. After all, what is a woman doing out on her own in the middle of the night when she is married? But I have a husband. And guess where he is? He is safely tucked up in our king-size bed, sleeping by now. He does the responsible things, like earn the money, and then he gets enough sleep so that he can feel fresh in the morning. I wish I were a man so I could be satisfied with this mundane banality. Narrow confinement could, I think, be fun. I would love my responsible sort of life. But I am a woman, so what do I do. I creep around at night to deliver packages to grandchildren for other people's grandmothers.'

He looked at her as she spoke. His Calvin Klein face said; buy me I will be sexy and durable underwear if you take me home. But then he did not know if she even liked sexy underwear. He thought that he liked Y. He thought that he liked her a lot. Maybe he was even falling in love. He wondered what she looked like without clothes on, maybe with a pair of Calvin Klein underpants. Would she just be naked, or would she be as beautifully naked as he wanted her to be?

'They never took their clothes off in the movie,' Freddie said. She knew what he was thinking. She wondered if she should explore this theme or if she should just let it be a short fantasy for him, a fantasy that he would forget as soon as he thought of X again.

'I wish I was a man so that I too could sleep well tonight,' he said.

Freddie nudged him. 'You are a man. I have already told you this,' she said to him.

'Oh well, I forgot,' he said. 'And you never tell me anyway. I never heard you say it before. You need to remind me. How can I read this book when I am in it, a character? You have to tell me. I can't read your mind.'

Y looked at him. Her expression said, 'I like you too, but I have other needs that I must attend to.'

'I think that I have to go now,' Y said. She looked at her watch. 'And anyway this waiter wants to put on his lullaby music and sleep. But I am glad that we met each other, twice now in one day – weird. Okay, cheers.'

He remained on the chair. Freddie sat next to him. There was no sound. A rat ran up the drainpipe that ran along the top of the building. Freddie looked at it. I wonder if it is a male or a female rat, she mused. Long whiskers protruded from its face. Then she noticed that it only had whiskers on the one side. Maybe someone had cut off the ones that used to grow on the other. Maybe someone had fallen out of love with this rat and bitten them off. It bumped into the wall as it ran. Whiskers keep a rat in balance, Freddie thought. They prevent it from bumping into things in the dark. Now that it only has whiskers on the one side of its face, it bumps into the wall. And rats are sentient so it must feel unhappy every time it bumps its face on the bricks. 'What are you so afraid of?' Freddie turned to him as the rat disappeared into the open end of the drain, the closed space where it no longer had to run and bump its face on the bricks of the wall.

'I am not sure,' he replied. 'Maybe I am just afraid as I do not know what will happen. I have no control over anything that I do or that is done around me. Maybe that is why I am afraid.'

'Well, I have control,' Freddie said. 'And would I do anything to harm you? Well, you do not know. The only thing that you do know is that your life is transient. When the pages of this book are written, when I have closed it, then you no longer exist. But while you are here, well, don't worry. And anyway, for what it is worth, it does not help to worry. Your anxiety will not make me write a longer novel. I will write for a day. The book will not end any more quickly or slowly, it will just end after a day.'

'But really, I am afraid that X no longer loves me.' He did not say these words aloud. But Freddie knew that this is what he was thinking. She knew because she was writing it. He did not fear his lack of control. He did not even fear the fact that soon he would be finished, his life ended. He feared, more than anything, X, his love for X. 'I wonder why I like her, this Y person,' he continued. 'Maybe it is because I think that we are both sacrificing something. But I do not know what it is. You know what it is.' He turned to Freddie. 'Tell me what it is, or just tell me that I am wrong. Maybe it is because neither of us is a man, and we want to be men. There is some kind of synergy between us. We both want something and we cannot have it.'

'Well, you do have it, remember,' Freddie said. 'And you only need to fear if you think that you have a future. Because a future means you have to keep on living. And you have no future beyond these pages, so don't fear. Come, let's go back to the hotel.'

They got up from the table. A shadow walked in front of them. It was a man. He seemed to grow from the mouldy walls of each building that he passed, his body blended into the brickwork. He was inanimate. He was cold. He was just the dark of a light. There was nothing that he needed to fear.

XIII

X did not have to drive far to get home, only a few kilometres. It was late and there were no cars on the road. An occasional person walked on the sidewalk – hatless, homeless. Where are they going to, he wondered. It is so late.

'They have already woken up and are going to work,' Freddie said to him. Well, work – that is if they have it. Otherwise they have woken up just for a day of very little. You, well, you still have the darkness ahead of you.'

X pressed the remote control button and the wooden garage door opened. He drove into the dark hole. It was a cave. He parked the car in just the right place, far enough away from the lawn mower but not too close to the wall. He could open the car door without scraping it. He got out. X looked at his watch. It glowed in the dark and said 12h45. He walked inside. The dog, which lay in the front garden, barked. He opened the sliding patio door. The golden dog jumped at him as if to say, 'Glad that you are here. It was getting lonely.'

Do dogs get lonely, Freddie wondered as she watched them. They probably do. That rat was a sentient creature, so the dog must also feel. But what is loneliness, she mused. Is it when you hate your own company? Is it when you have a memory of not being lonely, of having someone around to hold you? To hold you down.

X leaned over the golden fur. He put his arms around the dog's neck. X was lonely. X was alone. And X had memories of nights and days of not being alone. He walked towards the bedroom. He needed a shower. He wanted to shower the night away. He wanted to shower away what had happened. He did not want to see him again. All he caused were memories of a memory. Good for the time that it lasted, good for a short time. Goodness that was unreal. X had nothing.

There was a shrill buzz. X looked around him. 'It is the phone,' Freddie said to him. 'It should not be making a noise this early in the morning or this late at night, but it is the phone. That is what is making the sound.'

X turned around. He almost ran to the phone that was standing on a table in the entrance hall of the house. He grabbed it and held it upward towards his ear. He was afraid.

'It is not him, you fool,' Freddie said. 'Why would he call you? Besides he does not even know your name so how could he know your telephone number?' But X feared that he would find him out. X feared that maybe he was a fraud. X knew that he was a fraud.

X held the phone to his right ear. 'Yes,' he said. He heard a voice but there was loud laughter and music in the background. The voice was faint and whispered.

'X,' he heard.

'Speak louder. I can't hear who it is,' X said into the telephone.

'X,' and then he recognised the voice. It was Y. 'X, I need some help. X, I need you to come get me.'

'Where are you?' he said. There was a shiver in his voice. It fell downwards. The music rose upwards. It was getting louder and she was getting softer.

'I need help. I need R1000. Come and get me. Please come and fetch me. I can't get out without you.'

'She means,' Freddie said, 'she can't get out without the money. It is not your human form that she needs.'

'X,' she said, 'I am in Berea in Soper Road – number 666. It is a block of flats called Eugenie Court and I am on the sixth floor – number 666. Please fetch me. Please.' Then there was a click. The whirr of the receiver told X that she had put the telephone down. The line was dead.

'What the fuck must I do? What the fuck must I do?' X was scared. He knew Soper Road in Berea had a reputation for strong-armed violence. He had not been there for a long time. The last time he had been there was when he visited his grandmother – a little old lady who lived in one of the hotels that lined the street, 'residential hotels', they called them. He remembered how these little old ladies lined the road under the large pine trees that shaded it. These little old ladies walked up the road with their baskets on their arms to Checkers. But he had not been there for a long time. He had not been there since the Africans had moved in. He had not been there since it became mandatory for the cashiers at the supermarket checkout counters to speak French. He had not been there since all the little old ladies had died. X was scared.

'You must go,' said Freddie. 'You have to go. This is the person that you are supposed to care about. This is the person who you take care of. You have to show a little bit of bravery even though it is a sham, even though it is all bullshit. Take the dog. Maybe it will make you feel better. Maybe it will make you feel more secure. The dog will be your gun, a domesticated gun.' X was pale. Maybe it is just the light in this room, thought Freddie. Surely he can't be pale already. He has not even left the suburbs.

X took out a wallet. It was kept safely in his back pocket. He counted the money in it. He had the R1000; he had drawn money from the bank teller earlier in the day – money for the wages that he had to pay the domestic worker. He put his wallet on the table and put the money into his jacket pocket, inside his jacket near his shirt. The green and red and brown notes lay near his heart and moved up and down as the arteries drove the blood to his head. Then X took off his watch. It was not an expensive watch, but he thought that he should look plain. He should have nothing on him that could be taken by anyone. Reluctantly, he went out the door and towards the garage. For an instant he hesitated, then he turned back again. He opened the door and whistled for the golden dog, the dog that knew only the smells of a suburban green garden. The dog came to him, his tail moving from side to side. A smear of mud defiled the white wall.

'Come,' said X, 'we are going to a war zone.' Once again he walked to the garage. Both of them got into the white car, the dog and the man. Then he drove down the road. Freddie watched the car as it faded into the distance. There were no lights in the road outside the house. The lamps had disappeared. It was a black and white picture.

X drove into Berea. He drove along its outskirts at first, not wanting to drive through Hillbrow. Then he turned the wheel of the car. I had better do it, he thought. I can't *not* do it. He drove down Tudhope Road and then turned right into Soper Road. Lights from the flats crept onto the sidewalk. From one of the hotels, one where he remembered buying a drink in a white bar, 'The Mark', rap music spilled. A different sound became a drone.

Strange, Freddie thought as she listened, music has become one big sound. Nothing is discernible anymore. Music comes through the speakerphones that sit on the bar counter. It comes from the radio that plays in the car. No one listens to music anymore. It is accessible to all. It is just one sound that is always available.

Outside the 'Mark Hotel' there were bodies on the pavement. X did not look at the people who wore the clothing that walked with them. X could not look sideways, so he looked ahead, straight ahead. There was a palpable fear in the air. A strange and filthy smell surrounded X even though the windows of the car were tightly wound up. He wondered what it was. Could it be that the dirt in the street could reach its tentacles into the car? Could it be the dog beside him? Could it be his own fear that he smelt?

'Yes,' Freddie said to him, 'it is you. You smell of fear, and fear has a terrible stench. The stench keeps away the wild and the vicious. That is why you smell. Put your nose into the fur of the dog, you will find that it does not smell. The dog is not afraid... yet.'

X looked carefully at the numbers. There were so few of them that he had to count each building. Each block of flats with no numbers on it had to be counted before he moved onto the next one. Then he saw the seven-storied building. The words 'Eugenie Court' were painted on the wall. An awning that no longer provided shade for anyone hung over the entrance. The letters were black. The wall was a miserable yellow, like vomit in a toilet. The 'g' from 'Eugenie' had been erased.

It was late. A lot of men stood outside the building. They just waited there silently in small insect-like groups – flies. Some of them looked like they should be in a smart Johannesburg nightclub. They wore dark leather jackets and black denim jeans. A few of them wore mirrored sunglasses. They were all shameful.

Like the American movies, thought Freddie. Like those African American guys from Harlem. I suppose they did not have mirrored sunglasses in Casablanca. They had not yet been invented.

All of the men looked and listened. They listened for sirens and watched for police cars. X looked at the groups again. He peered out of the window.

'Yes,' said Freddie, 'you are right; it is what you think it is.'

X saw a gun taken out of a jacket pocket. The man who held it caressed it gently, an injured bird – something that needed to be taken care of. He opened the gun and poured the yellow bullets onto the palm of his hand. One by one he counted them. He traced his fingers over the blunt bullet tips. Then he put them tenderly back into the barrel of the gun. He placed the metal back in his pocket and patted it. Then he pulled out a calculator. For a while he pressed at the numbers. A white Porsche glided up the street. X could see the window slowly move downwards. The man did not move. He pressed the buttons. A light from above shone down on his head. He was in a spotlight. He was behind a camera. It was the way he posed. His mouth opened wide as he laughed and turned to speak, his head thrown backwards as he laughed. The Porsche did not move.

The dog next to X began to whine. 'Shhh,' said X, 'don't make a noise.'

'What difference does it make?' said Freddie. 'There are such sounds in the street that a dog's howl would just add to the music with no features.'

A white hand moved out of the window of the Porsche. The man with the calculator stopped speaking and put the instrument back into his pocket. He took out a small packet from his jacket and held it next to the hand, but he did not give it over. Two hands hovered above each other. They spoke. The hand in the Porsche drew in and touched the steering wheel of the car. The Porsche moved a little further down the street and stopped. The hand appeared once more. This time it had the dirt of money in it. From somewhere another body appeared and took the notes from the hand. Now another pair of hands held money. Both hands moving at once counted the notes. An inanimate head nodded and the Porsche reversed slowly.

'They are counting money in this street,' thought X.

'Well, who can you trust now?' said Freddie.

A black hand met with a white hand, and in a swirl the packet was transferred from one hand to another. And the Porsche drove away. Its wheels left a skid mark on the tar, the dirt on a grave.

X parked the car. He opened the door and put his right leg on the pavement. His black leather shoes stepped into a puddle of vomit. It was green; expensive vomit for expensive shoes. And then the men were around him. He did not know why they were around him. What had he done that they wanted to get to him? A leather mask glowed in the half-lit street. It laughed at X.

'You are such a fool,' said Freddie. 'Remember the Porsche. They think you want to make some purchases.'

'I need to find a girl,' said X as he drew in his leg and closed the door. The vomit smelt bad. He locked the door and wound the window down. 'I need to go up,' and he pointed at the block of flats. 'Sixth floor... a girl.'

Why do white men always talk to black men as if they are

talking to children or people who do not speak English, Freddie thought. Well, I suppose that some of these people don't speak English. Maybe they speak French. People are condemned if they do not speak the language that you speak. I wonder if there are injurious associations between the language a person speaks and acts of delinquency. I sort of think that there must be. X has his prejudice reinforced when the prospective delinquency is Y and drugs, and the language is foreign.

'White girl,' said X. The golden dog growled as a black hand entered the window. X opened the door and got out of the car. The dog jumped after him. X pointed upwards. 'A girl,' he said, his voice hysterical. Then he took some money from his pocket and pointed upwards again. 'The white girl... I pay.' The men laughed as one. They moved to create a Red Sea pathway, but X was not Moses. X walked to the entrance of the building. The dog followed him. Someone shouted, but X did not turn around to see who it was and what he shouted at. He walked straight into the building. X never turned around. He never looked back, ever.

There was a lift ahead of him. But the lift did not work. X looked around; there was a flight of stairs to the right of the door. He ran up them. Up and up and up and up. Six flights. The sound of dog's paws next to him beat time to the rap music outside, a sad sound of soles on concrete. Then X was on the sixth floor. The door of a flat was open.

'Yes,' said Freddie, 'that's it, number 666. Go inside.' She wondered what X would do as she spoke. X, the Brave – now he was brave, for he was numb – walked inside. The dog followed him. Golden paws on black and white linoleum.

A faecal stain limped down a wall. The golden dog ran to lick it. A dim light shone down from a socket. There was no bulb in it; instead a torch was hooked into where the bulb should be. By the window, under the pool of torchlight, was Y. The shadow of the moon behind a cloud played on the empty Coke can that lay on the floor. X looked at her and saw that she was wearing the same clothes that she had been wearing that morning. They were dirty; the white shirt was now grey.

Its buttons were loose, some had even been torn off it. In the light she looked sallow. Y looked up at him. Then she looked at the big man who stood over her. X was certain that he had seen this man before. His muscles bulged from his tight T-shirt. In his ear was a golden earring.

'You have seen him before,' said Freddie. 'He is in that show, what is it now, *New York City Undercover*. Except that there he is the good guy. Here he is a drug dealer. There he catches those guys that buy and sell the drugs. Roles can always be changed, like the clothes that you wear.'

'Give it to me,' Y said. X heard the voice. He did not turn around but stared at the man who he had seen on television. He wondered if he had ever seen a star before.

'Hurry up,' Y said. 'Give it to me.' X turned to look at Y. She drew on her cigarette. Smoke curled from its tip. Her fingers were yellow in the dim light.

I wonder if they are nicotine-stained, those fingers, X thought. It would be a pity as she has such beautiful fingers. Piano-playing fingers.

The man from *New York City Undercover* spoke in a husky low voice. 'I am owed the money, not you, you fucking white bitch. You got the white powder. I get the money. Otherwise you can get down on your knees again and I'll fuck you and that dog that he brought with him.' The golden earring leant backwards and scratched the dog between its ears. His nails were clean and manicured. The dog nuzzled him gently in the groin. 'Even the dog will be better than you, clean… a clean hole.' He laughed.

I wonder if they censor this kind of talk in *New York City Undercover*, X thought. Kids watch it. I have never heard them speak like this before.

'Children just watch what goes on around them,' said Freddie. 'They learn to speak because this is what they hear. You can censor it all if you want to, but they hear it in this world anyway. Boy kids will always be photographed from below and girl kids, well they will be photographed from above – that's listening.'

END

X looked at the man from the television show. He craned his neck and looked upwards. The man was tall. He was high.

'Give it to him, X,' she said, 'then I can finish my cigarette in peace without him punching me all the time. Then we can go home, or somewhere.'

'Give it to me.' X heard the stereo voice again, an expensive stereo recording. X turned around. In the shadows he saw a black hand. On the fourth finger there was a ring. It may have been a wedding band, or else it may have been used to rip out a piece of skin. It could be both of these things. He passed the money to the hand.

'I did not have enough fucking cash,' Y said, 'so he said if I did not pay he would keep me here. I would need an exit visa to get out. I would need an exit visa signed by the chief of the police and I don't think that he would sign one of those for me.' She laughed. 'You see, X, it would be his duty to see to it that I stayed here and paid off my debt. Maybe I could sleep with the chief of police. Then he would sign a visa for me. But I suppose I fuck like anyone else so that would not be enough. Nothing different. Should I take you with me? How do you fuck? I can't remember.' She laughed again, this time baring her teeth as she laughed.

'It is not them that she bares her teeth for,' said Freddie. 'It's you... X.' He is actually very sexy, the man from the television show. 'Why are you looking so down?' Freddie turned to X, but Y broke in before X could say anything.

'And what the fuck did you bring the dog for, X?' She reached over to stroke its golden head. She squashed the cigarette out on the floor grinding it in the shadow of the moon beneath her shoe.

I wish that moon shadow were that fucker's television eyes, *New York City Undercover* television eyes, thought X. 'Come, let's go, he's got his money now.'

The stereo voice in the corner laughed and said, 'Get out. Get out, lady. I will call you the lady and the man with the money. Get out of here lady and the man with the money.'

The dog looked at the man and wagged his tail. It barked at the television image. Then it turned and followed X and Y from the room.

XIV

'I wonder what we will have tonight,' said the policeman in the blue uniform. 'Rosebank is not like the townships. Nothing really happens here. At least something happens in the townships.' He yawned as he shuffled the papers on the desk. He thought about his wife and his children at home. How many children do I have, he thought. He often had to count them on his fingers. One, two, three... They are watching the Brady Bunch on television at this time. He looked at his watch. Great show – wish I could watch it now. He yawned again and thought about the time before he was posted to this station, the time that he spent in Alexandra Township.

'Tell me about it,' said Freddie. 'Why not? I have to fill up the pages somehow, so I may as well get your story.'

The policeman got up from his desk and walked to the coffee machine. He pushed a button and a polystyrene cup slid out of a black hole. Then there was the sound of water pouring and the steam rose. White coffee, black with something milky, filled the cup; the policeman watched the liquid. He remembered the month before. Black, lots of black – blacks, *kaffirs*.

The tank lurched forward. It was heavy and the road that it travelled on was covered in holes. The rain fell from the sky. It was metallic and cloudy. The drops rattled on the iron outsides of the machine. He peered through the porthole. It was so small that he could only see a small grey patch in front of him. But they were there, all of them. Their black-and-white school uniforms stood out of the moving rain. Their hair was wet and, because it was short and dark and very curly, it was not plastered down. The drops just sat on the top of it. They balanced in a curled tightrope and they shone. Blacks, he thought, there are so many blacks.

'Say a prayer,' said Freddie. 'They have stones in their hands, those blacks, and you have a tank, which you are inside. Say a prayer – your guns may not be as strong as their stones.'

He looked out of the hole again. A boy held a stone in his hand. He raised his hand as if he was going to throw the stone at the tank. The policeman ducked his head below the porthole; he wondered if the stones could penetrate the heavy metal. There was smoke in the air. It was raining. It was grey. He did not know why or how a fire could keep alight in this weather.

'It's because it's a movie,' said Freddie.

The children continued to run down the rickety road. The tank continued to follow them. He heard the shouts. 'Viva ANC... Viva Nelson Mandela... Mayibuye Africa...'

Those fucking blacks, they just want to bring this country down, he thought. They just want the fucking terrorists to come in here and mess things up. They want the devil in this hell.

The crowd of children stopped running. They gathered in front of the tank. He heard the voice of his captain: 'All we want is to check your documents. That is all we are here for. We don't want to get violent.' The tank lurched to a halt. 'Get out, all of you,' the captain said. 'Search them. Look for illegals, look for guns and ammunition, look for terrorists. There must be some of them here. Scum. Scum... fucking *kaffirs*.' He climbed from the tank. He felt the rain run down his back where it had fallen into his jacket. The water moved down his back and over a boil that he felt growing there.

He thought about his wife and how only that morning she had squeezed it. He was lying face down on the bed. He was naked. She said, 'Andre, a pimple. I think I must squeeze it.' And he had just kept lying still. He just lay there while he felt her hands on his back. It was painful. It felt good. He liked pain... sometimes. He felt his cock stir between his legs.

'Ouch, shit, fuck it,' he said as he felt her squeeze and heard her gasp. Then he saw the pus fly from the pimple and land on the front of the mauve dressing gown that his wife was wearing. A third nipple, only it was yellow – a Chinese nipple.

You did not really see the pus, thought Freddie. How could you? It was behind you all the time. Maybe *I* saw it. It was yellow and had a bad smell. It smelt like rotting flesh. It smelt like the flesh of the dead. And the pus was sticky.

Fabulous, he thought, I like my wife to squeeze my pimples. He put his hand behind him and felt the bumps on his back. He had so many of them. Pimples covered his back like a sequined cloth. At least I no longer have them on my face, he thought. He got up from the bed. He looked at his wife. Her dressing gown fell open as he walked past her. He put his hand inside it and felt her cunt. It was dry. In the bathroom he looked in the mirror. His face was scarred.

And the water moved over the hillock on his back and travelled downwards towards his anus. He felt the gun in his hand; he had better make sure he could use it quickly, he thought. He looked down and saw that it was loaded. If he just touched the trigger lightly a bullet would spin from its barrel. The blacks across from him still shouted. They did not fear his gun. He walked up to one of the children, a man really; he must have been about fourteen. 'May I see your papers,' he said. He thought to himself as he spoke, it is best to be polite here. My mother told me that a Christian is always polite, even to animals. He approached the boy. He held his gun to his chest. 'Your papers,' he said again.

'I don't have them on me,' the boy said.

'Well, in that case, you had better just step to that side so that we can take you in,' he said to him.

The boy patted his trouser pockets. 'Wait, it is just possible that I... maybe I do have them, maybe they are here.' He pulled out a dirty piece of what used to be white paper.

They can't even keep their white things white, the policeman thought. He took the paper as the rain melted the ballpoint writing on it. He looked closely at the writing. 'These are not papers for you,' he said. 'They are papers for someone else, someone who is sixty years old, and anyway they have expired. You can't be in the city.'

Suddenly the boy laughed and started to run. 'Stop,' the policeman screamed. 'Stop!' He lifted his gun. The boy looked back at him and laughed again. Then the policeman pulled the trigger. He felt the gun kick into his hand, his wrist snap, and the bullet move forward. The boy fell to the ground. The crowd shouted, the crowd cried salty tears.

'Let's get out of here,' he heard his captain say. 'Hurry. Close the tank door after you.' He jumped into the tank and felt the metal hatch close him in. He felt fine now, now that he had killed an animal. The tank began to move forward; bump, bump, he felt it as it rode over the body.

The tank driver laughed at him and said, 'Well, here it goes again. Cheers, we are having a real good time.' He felt the tank gears grind into reverse and then he felt it again; bump bump.

He smiled at the driver. Squash the fucking shit out of him. He looked backwards from the porthole and saw another black – maybe he was a child – run over and lift the dead boy into his arms. The head and feet tilted downwards towards the earth. Then the boy began to run down the road. He was crying. He was a brother. The water flashed on his face.

'Well,' said Freddie, 'that is a fine atrocity story. Now tell us about the Brady Bunch and what you want your kid to be when he is all grown up. Atrocity stories are always the same. They always sound the same. The same words are used. The Brady Bunch – mmm – do these stories evoke a feeling of outrage? It is all just the same, but I suppose that poor boy was still gripped by the illusion that it all meant something. In fact he probably believed that he died for a cause. His mother and father, if they are still alive, will also think this. He will become a martyr. Think of his headstone, think of his grave, think of the politicians who will travel to the cemetery to remember his grave. Maybe they will even leave a rose behind on the head stone, a memorial. Now,' Freddie turned to the policeman, 'tell us a little about how kind you can be, how you have sentimentality in you.'

The policeman leaned back in his chair – the front legs lifted off the ground – and thought about this question. Freddie could almost see his thoughts. They balanced on two back legs as he rocked.

He opened his mouth. It was in a house in Bryanston, a white area north of the city. It was a plain house. Nothing about it was suspicious. But we had had a tip off that something illegal was going on there. So one night we went along. It was about midnight when thirty of us leopard crawled across the mowed green grass. We tried to find a window that did not have a curtain over it. And then I found a slit, a small slit in the material where the curtains had not been properly closed. I called to the captain, 'You can see inside from here', and together we looked into the room. In it were people and a roulette table. The silver ball made a clinking sound as the wheel spun.

'Now... now,' shouted the captain, 'now... Let's go in and get the fuckers... dishonest shits.'

He broke down the wooden doors that led into the kitchen. Another policeman smashed the glass of a window. And they crashed into the room where the wheel was spinning fire.

The policeman and his colleagues rounded up some of the people. They were all white, they were all people. Then they joined in the fun. 'A bit of money on the side of the paycheque never harmed anyone,' the policeman said to Freddie.

Blue uniforms and Bryanston patrons played the wheel. The croupier spun and down went the chips, on the black squares, on the white squares, on the red squares. Plastic on the table makes a harsh sound.

A woman came up to the policeman. She was pretty and plain; she had dark hair that caressed her shoulders. She was about twenty.

'Can I speak to you?' she asked him. He felt surprised, he felt flattered. 'Why did she want to speak to him?'

'Please,' she said, 'you look as if you have a kind heart. I think that maybe, maybe you can help me. I am here with my husband. He is from a farm in the Eastern Cape and he has come to Johannesburg to find a job. People where we lived said that he was certain to get a job on the railways. They give jobs to white boys on the railways. And Jan, well he has no skill. He cannot even read properly. And the captain,' she pointed to his captain, his police captain, 'well, the captain said, the captain said that he could help us if I... What kind of the man is the captain, Sir? Tell me, please.'

'The captain is just like any other man, only more so,' the policeman replied. 'He is broadminded. He thinks a lot.'

'We need money. We have nowhere to stay. My husband, well, he is trying to win something at roulette and of course he is losing,' she continued.

'How long have you been married?' the policeman asked her. He thought of his own wife and how he lived so that he could protect and provide for her. He wondered what she was doing just at that minute. Was she waiting for him so that he could fuck her in the rough dark night? 'How long have you been married?' he repeated.

'Eight weeks. Things are very bad in the Eastern Cape. A devil has the people by the throat; the blacks kill us and steal our things. So Jan and I, well, we do not want our children to grow up on that farm.'

'So you decided to come here to Johannesburg,' he said.

'Yes, but we have no more money. The travelling was so expensive and difficult. It cost much more than we thought to get here. And then the captain...' She looked around the room searching for the captain '... and then the captain, he said I should meet him here tonight and, well, he wants to help us. He said that maybe Jan could get a job in the police, but we have nothing, except...'

'And you want to know from me whether he will keep his word,' the policeman asked.

'Oh yes, will he keep his word? And also, Sir, you are a man. If your wife loved you so much so that your happiness was the only thing that she wanted in the whole world, but she did a bad thing to make certain of it. Could you forgive her?'

The policeman looked at her. 'No,' he said, 'I could not forgive her. Go back to the farm.'

'But it means so much to us,' she continued. 'We needed to leave and come to the city. And if Jan should find out, he is only a boy. In many ways I am so much older than he is.'

'Yes, well, we all have problems in Johannesburg,' the policeman said. He got up and walked towards the roulette table. The policemen laughed and put their chips on the squares. He walked up to a man who spun the wheel and whispered into his ear. The man looked at him and laughed. 'Put your money on the red squares,' the policeman said to Jan, 'and keep it there.' The wheel spun and spun and spun in the dry air. The chips grew and grew and grew. 'Cash them in and hurry,' the policeman said to Jan. 'Get out because we are soon going to close this place and arrest everybody.' The young girl looked at him. 'He is just a lucky guy,' the policeman said to her and walked away.

'Not a bad story,' said Freddie. 'Could have been more visual, but it is touching.'

'Well, that was last month, or was it the month before?' the policeman said. 'Maybe Alexandra township was last month. Now, here I sit, and there is not a black in sight, not even a fucking pretty girl from the Eastern Cape.' He picked up the file that had fallen to the floor and opened it. A notice stared out at him. The writing was black. 'To all officers in the South African Police force in Rosebank. Two policemen murdered in Berea in a drug bust. Murderer and possible accomplices – one of them a well-dressed white woman with blonde hair – possibly heading for the suburbs, possibly in the Rosebank area. Round up all suspicious characters and search them for drugs.'

Well, he thought, at least it's something to do. Strange that a white woman is involved in this type of thing. She should have a husband to keep her busy. He got up and left his chair. He walked out of the room and into an area where several other policemen gathered. 'Come, let's go. Maybe we should search the hotels in the area. Let's start with the Rosebank Hotel. Let's bust the bar there. Weirdos hang out in that place. And keep a lookout for a white woman with blonde hair. She is part of the drug gang.' He picked up the cup that was lying on the desk. The dregs of the coffee lay at the bottom of the chipped polystyrene cup. The policeman leaned over and opened the top drawer of his desk. He took out a half bottle of brandy. He poured an inch into the white coffee and drank it in a gulp.

'I am a policeman,' he said to Freddie, as he felt the heat of the brandy bravely gather around the hair on his chest. 'I have never faced the yellow saliva-dripping mouth of a buffalo with a gun in my hands, but I have faced a sweating black. I have never felt the hot fetid breath of a lion as I move in to shoot it in the heart, but I have felt the breath of a black wheeze as I shoot at his ragged chest. I do not know what an injured leopard sounds like as it whispers to its friends, "I am done for", but I know the sound that a black makes as he cries out with his pain. But I do not know what it feels like to kill a human being.' He felt a tremor in his breast. He felt eager. His hands shook. He felt the adrenalin start to wind its way through his veins. Maybe. Just maybe?

'You look very excited,' said Freddie. 'You feel the lure of the hunt. Maybe this time you will find action, real death. You might kill a person tonight.'

XV

'Come,' Y said, 'let's go out and get a drink, together. You must want to find something, even if it's just a whisky.'

X looked at his wife. She looked sexy in the evening light. He wondered if the picture was just his picture, or if it was the light, or if it was Y herself.

She looked at him. Come, I do love you. X looked at Y again and knew why he loved her. Her yellow hair was clean now; it fell over her forehead in straight strips. Her mouth was scarlet; it was smothered in lipstick – a scarlet letter on her face. Her thin frame was covered in blue denim and her arms were bare. She still had a little bit of muscle left in her arms. They were curved. Maybe she just looked a little older than she was ten years ago. Maybe if you looked closely you could see the fine lines around her mouth and the wrinkled skin above her eyes. But X did not look closely. He was still in love with her. He could not look closely, just as he had never looked closely at anyone.

'Okay,' X said. 'What about the Rosebank Hotel? It is not far and they have great cocktails.' He knew as he said this that he wanted to find him again. Maybe he would not as he had already gone back to Maputo. He did not know, but he wanted to be in the same space. He wanted to feel the heat in a cushion of the chair where he may have sat. He wanted to feel the curve of his back.

'Rosebank Hotel it is,' Y said.

If X had not suggested this, Y would have, thought Freddie. I can't intervene in this show. But I know that Y must be in Rick's Café tonight.

The courier is supposed to be there tonight, Y thought to herself. I wonder if he has the stuff. All I have to do is see him and give him the correct sign. And anyway I love those cocktails. She laughed at X. What did he know about cocktails? Y picked up her bag; it was a large one. She put it over her shoulder. X followed her from the house to the garage, while Freddie wondered if tonight the golden dog would be left behind.

Rick's Café was full that night. 'Everyone comes to Rick's,' Freddie said to X. 'Even you.' The same man sat at the piano and played late-night movie songs. The same barman mixed the cocktails, ate the olives and poured the whisky. The same waiters wore red gloves and served the drinks. They had the same servile and ingratiating look on their faces. 'They have not been fired,' said Freddie. 'The management here must be liberal, or maybe they are just nervous and confused about the rise of the newly allowed union or maybe they know that all the foreign journalists stay here when they come to Johannesburg. Whatever they are, it is easier to write about the same faces because then I do not have to describe new ones. Not that I described the old ones. Nameless faceless people. Nameless, faceless, nothing.'

X did not remember what had happened the night that he had last been in Rick's Café. He could only remember him. He could only remember the smell of the whisky on the bedroom table. He could only remember his voice – not the words, just the sound of the voice. He could only remember his lips on his lips. He remembered wiping the lipstick stain from them with a tissue – not his handkerchief, but a tissue – before he returned home.

The weasel man still sat at his table. He was dressed differently tonight, but, thought Freddie, I can still describe him as a weasel. At least then you will know to whom I am referring.

Y looked around the room. 'Get me a whisky,' she said to X. 'I just want to sit here and look at all these self-satisfied people.' X left the table and walked to the bar. The barman smiled at him, a practised smile. His white teeth shone in his black face. Around his neck he wore a white medallion held on a black string. The medallion was made of ivory. X ordered his drinks then he moved back to the table. Y was looking around the room when he returned. Then she saw the weasel-like man. 'Seen a man that I know,' she said to X. 'Let me just go and chat to him for a second.'

X frowned. Who would she know here tonight? But more than this he just wanted to spend the evening like old times. Just talking and staring into each other's eyes, noticing no-one, just each other. Then later, well later they would do what they used to do.

Y walked over to the weasel. She opened her bag and took out a plastic cigarette lighter. Then she took a cigarette from a packet. She looked at the weasel and flicked the lighter. No flame appeared. She flicked it again, still no flame. 'Excuse me, do you have a match or a lighter?' she said to the weasel. 'This one does not seem to work anymore and I could have sworn that I filled it with gas just the other day.' She smiled at him.

He smiled back at her. His sharp teeth were nicotine-stain yellow. 'Don't think so.' He answered without looking into her eyes.

'Perhaps you know someone who does have a match,' Y continued. She was sure it was the weasel. There were no other weasels in the bar. 'Look at this lighter and see if you can get it to work.' She bent down and held the lighter out to him. He looked up and took it. He saw the picture in the plastic. It was a man drinking Coke, or rather the words on the picture said Coca-Cola, but he knew what it meant.

'Oh yes, maybe I do, now that I am thinking straight,' he said to Y, and took out a box of matches from his pocket. The man turned and looked over his shoulder. He saw X walking across the floor towards them. 'This match seems not to work. I will find another. Meet me outside the men's toilet in ten minutes.'

'Your drink is on the table,' said X. 'Shall I bring it to you?'

'No,' said Y, 'I will come with you.' X and Y walked back

to their table. She looked worried.

'Don't be worried,' Freddie said to her. 'Worry will not change anything, so what is the point? All it will do is make you bite your nails.'

Y sat down and took a sip of the whisky from her glass. X raised his before putting the glass to his lips. 'Cheers,' he said.

'Oh, I forgot, you like to clink glasses. Cheers,' she replied. For a minute she thought, and then she raised her glass again and said, 'To life and maybe love.' She took out her lighter and lit a cigarette. The plastic lighter, with the picture of the man who drank a Coca-Cola on it, flared. A flame glowed. Y held the lighter to her cigarette. She inhaled and then she blew smoke from her nostrils. A short while later she got up. 'Must go to the toilet. Be back in a minute.'

X sighed. Freddie sat and watched them. There was nothing for her to describe. There were no butterflies, there was no azure sea. Rick's Café was prosaic. There was nothing but the sound of the piano.

Tick, tock, tick, tock... Time is fleeting, madness takes its toll, how does the rest of the song go? And soon this story will end... Tick, tock, tick, tock... time goes by... After time comes time...

At the toilet door the weasel looked at Y. 'You sure are a sexy bitch,' he said. 'The lighter, can I see it again?'

She took the lighter from her bag. She moved the thumb of her right hand. A flame shot forward. 'Give it to me. It is paid for; you know that they have already paid you.' Y held the flame close to the weasel's face. She smelt a hair burn. 'And stop irritating me.'

'A big girl are we?' he said. A smirk covered his face. 'It is in the piano, the left hand side, just under the lid. What the fuck do you think? Think that I would carry it around with me and get caught?'

Y hated this weasel for a moment. She looked at him and

walked back to where X sat. 'Remember when we first met,' she said to him, 'remember that song that we always used to play? *It had to be you...*' She hummed the notes.

X looked at her. He was grateful, grateful to Y for forging a link to the past. 'Yes,' he replied, 'yes, I remember it. I wonder if this man knows how to play it.'

'Let me go and ask him,' Y said and touched X on his cheek. Then she ran her hands down his neck. She stood up and began to move towards the piano.

'It is just like old times,' thought X.

The door to the bar swung open. Twenty men in blue stood there. 'We are raiding this place,' one of them shouted. 'All of you, sit. Don't move.' Guns trained down on Rick's Café. A policeman blew a loud blast on a whistle. Maybe this could be like Alexandra township, he thought, except here there are people. He drew the gun from his hip.

Y sat down quickly. The weasel looked up at the descending policemen. He got up. His hands were deep inside his pockets. They dug deeper and deeper. One of the policemen approached him.

'I wonder how he knew which person to search so quickly,' Freddie said.

'Come with me,' the policeman said to him.

'Can I just finish my drink?' the weasel said. He picked up his glass with the brown liquid in it. Suddenly he got up and began to run. 'It's her,' he shouted, and pointed at Y. 'She's the courier; ask her where the fucking stuff is.'

A fat policeman grabbed him from behind. The weasel struggled as he tried to break free. Another policeman looked to where the weasel pointed and his eyes focused on Y. She sat on her chair, her back straight. X reached over and took her hand. The fat policeman struggled with the weasel, but he escaped. A small bag fell from his jacket pocket. 'It's hers.' Again he pointed at Y. 'I was keeping it for her.' And then he ran.

'Stop! I will shoot you,' the policeman called out.

'With white people they are more polite,' Freddie said to X.

'They warn them if they intend to shoot.'

And the weasel ran. The sound of the bullet shouted in the muffled air. The weasel fell down slowly. The barman smiled as he watched. For him it was just another night. But tonight a white man was shot, not a black man. The blood stained the carpet red. It was the same colour as the blood that ran the streets in Alexandra township.

Red, like the sky at night, red like the ruby the Indian nurse wore in her nose, red, red...

X sat still. A young policeman approached Y. 'Let me look at what you have on you,' he said.

'You can look in my bag if you want to.' She smiled at him, a buttercup smile. He melted. 'I wonder what that man was doing pointing at me, very strange. Darling, do you know him?' She looked at X. The melting policeman opened her big bag and turned the contents onto the table. Tampax, lipstick, tissues, cigarettes and the Coca-Cola cigarette lighter fell out.

'Sorry, Madam,' the young policeman said. He was red, the colour of a man's face when a woman rejects him and when he has an erection. The policeman touched the front of his trousers. The blue cloth loomed large in front of him. X looked at him, and then he looked at the trousers that were now stretched. X wanted to cry.

The policeman who had read the notice in the station came up to the table. 'I think it's this woman,' he said. 'The description is right. But not today. We will get her some day. Get the details from him,' and he pointed at X. 'That must be the husband.' The policeman sounded incredulous. 'Let's clean up this mess.' He looked at Y and she smiled at him. But he did not get an erection; he was not aroused by her smile. 'I have been given a tip about a woman,' he said viciously, as he thought about the pimples on his back. 'I will get to you when I know for certain it is you. A white woman...' He spat at the floor. He was smug. He put his hand inside his shirt and squeezed another pimple that grew on his chest. It was large, a nipple. Then, as he pushed at it harder he felt it spit. A stain started to grow on the blue of the shirt.

'I wonder when this production will be over,' said Freddie.

XVI

I get solipsistic when I have to sit down for long periods and write, Freddie thought as her fingers clicked on the computer keyboard. It is always said that the life of a writer is solitary. Burroughs said that writers are like insects – without lives. Like sailors, people without human relationships. I am not sure about this observation. People surround me: policemen, drug dealers, X, Y, my character. They surrounded Burroughs too. There are times when they comfort me, when the language that they use, or the words that I use, keep me thinking, not about myself, but about them. They live in the words. I have relationships with them. Or if I want to I can be alone, they can be deleted. There will be no trace of them left, dead. And then there are other times when I am just writing the story – nothing in the words except the letters of the alphabet. Mysterious, meaningless syllables that only a few can understand. And if they understand them they can make them into images; a tree... a person... a picture. The computer screen lit up. She inserted the disk on which the whole story was saved. Relationships... intangible... on a disk. But the time is short, she thought as she looked at the screen.

X drove Y and himself home. All the way to the suburbs she laughed. She laughed at X, she laughed at the policeman, she laughed at the barman, she laughed at the dead weasel. X did not understand what it was that she laughed at. He felt trapped. Trapped in a story from which he could not escape.

'The credits have already been written – for the end of the movie that is,' Freddie said to him as he pulled into the garage.

'You have to just do this. You have no other alternative. Maybe when it is over you can go back to your colourless existence. And then you can comfort yourself by saying that the story was just a movie – one that you happened to go and watch, something that you did not intend to pay for. Would you sleep with a boy? Not in your kind of life. You are not a queer boy, or are you?' Freddie looked at him as she spoke. She looked amused. 'You are not a queer boy. You do not think you are, but I can make you into one if I want to. And I have wanted to, and I still want to. I want to make you boy/girl. Is there anything more than that you could possibly still want? Tell me. I'll give it to you.'

Y opened the car door and climbed out. X started to open the door. Then he hesitated. 'Think I have to go and see someone,' he said to her. 'Won't be very long. I just need to sort something out. You know that I am worried about you.'

'Worry if you want to,' she replied, 'but it won't change things. They will come and get me anyway. That is unless you do something about it. Ha... unless you do something about it. And you won't. What can you do? Your thoughts cannot extend far enough for you to think about what you could do. So I will just carry on. I will just sit and wait, so that maybe someday I will get out of here, or maybe I will have to sit in a tiny room with no plaster on the walls and a stinking latrine in the corner. I can fuck prison girls, girls in gangs. Won't that be a fantasy for you to dream on?'

As Y spoke X thought he heard the drone of an aeroplane overhead. It was flying low over their home. Then it cut its engines as if it was coming in to land. X started the car again and drove out of the garage, down the suburban street.

He caught the lift up to the third floor. No one in the reception area saw him – he had made certain of that. But why did he not want anyone to see him? He did not know and he did not think about it.

'You don't want them to see you because you think that someone like you would not do this. But they can see you anyway. They are watching a movie,' Freddie said to X. 'They are reading a book.'

X pushed the door of the room. It was not locked. It opened wide. The room was dark, but for an instant, as the light from the outside merged with the dark, X saw him seated at the window. The heart-shaped chocolate that he was starting to unwrap was in his fingers. He put it down on the table. 'How did you get in?' he said. He leaned forward to turn on the lamp. 'I wondered when you would come. I wondered how long it would be before the lipstick wore off and you needed some more of it.' He picked up the glass from the table. X saw that it was filled with whisky. He was always drinking in Johannesburg. Maybe he always drank in Mozambique, but X had never noticed this.

Freddie followed X into the room. She stretched out on the chair, which was placed before the television set. I suppose if you want to watch a movie it is nicer to lie down, she thought as she put her feet onto the coffee table. And then she watched them.

'When are you going back to Maputo?' X asked him.

'In two days time,' he replied. 'I have my air ticket right here.'

'I need help. I need someone to get onto that plane. She has to get onto it. She has to get out of here.'

'I suppose it is your wife who needs to get out,' he replied. 'I have been reading about your wife. The manuscript is not yet perfect. It is still in a rough draft, but the story is there.'

'Yes,' said X, 'she needs to get out of here fast or otherwise she will end up in jail. You can ask any price you want to. Just help her, please. And I want to stay with you,' X said. 'I will never be lonely again as long as I am here with you. I care about you and me,' X continued. 'You and I can be together.'

'You will have to do a little better than this,' he said. 'I need a bit more eloquence. Maybe you can tell me what a great woman she is. Maybe you can tell me what you used to feel for her. I use the words "used to feel". It sounds better. And it must be "used to feel" as you are being left behind.'

'She needs to be free,' X said. 'She needs to be free and

she is fighting for freedom. Freedom in the only thing that she knows about.'

'Ah,' he replied, 'freedom. What an important cause this freedom is.'

'You are, in your own way, fighting for it yourself,' X said to him. 'By writing your stories, those stories of an unjust war, you are fighting for freedom as well. It is the same thing.'

'I am no longer fighting for anything,' he said. 'Now I am only fighting for myself. I think that this is the only cause that I am interested in. We live alone, we die alone.'

'I think that I love you,' X said. 'I really think that I do. I remember the days that we spent in Xai Xai, I remember how…'

'I wouldn't bring up Xai Xai now if I were you,' he replied. 'It is poor salesmanship.'

X sat down on the bed. He could have used any other words but he used these ones. 'I love you. I still love you. I have always loved you. Just because I have hurt you don't take your revenge on me; don't take your revenge out on the world. If you don't help her she will surely die in prison.'

'What of it?' he replied. 'I am going to die in prison. We are all in a prison; there is no exit, although we will always search for a key. And prison is a good enough place to die in.'

X turned to look at the wall. 'Just help me. I still love you. Help me, I can no longer think.' He lay down on the bed and closed his eyes.

Freddie got up from the chair and turned on the television.

He walked over to the bed. X sat up and removed his shoes. Then he started to undo the buttons on X's shirt. He moved his hand down X's hairless chest. His fingers touched one of X's nipples. He felt it grow in his hands. He knelt down on the floor as X sat there. Giving head is often described as something where the recipient of the pleasure is dominant, he thought as he took X's cock in his mouth. Someone is always in a subservient position. I suppose that is what it looks like. Kneeling in front of a man. He sucked on the cock and it grew larger. But I am a man. And when I kneel I am kneeling because I have the power to give or not to give. He carefully peeled down X's trousers and pulled them off the inert body. He did not take his mouth from the cock that it ate. Smart office trousers – black with perfect creases down the sides of them – not the khaki pants of the beach. The symbol of growth that makes a man, he thought as his tongue caressed the glands in the head of the cock. It felt pink and fleshy under his saliva-covered tongue. He lifted his head from where it was deep in X's groin.

'I will do the thinking here,' he said to X. 'I will think and you will just respond. And then when I am done we can consider this love thing that you speak about.' He bent his head again, and then he stopped and smiled. He leaned over and Freddie passed him a book that was lying on the table next to the bed. We can do things that we would never have thought of. We can do things that are only described in a book. He started to read. Freddie watched the screen.

'... *Despite the fact that Durand is almost fifty, Juliette declares herself well satisfied with the exchanges and denies that she regrets murdering Clairwil. The two women, having reaffirmed how alike they are in mind and passions, indulge in vigorous sexual relations; Juliette confessing that she never had dealings with a woman who so thoroughly commanded the arts of imparting physical pleasure. They drink a good deal and Durand suggests that they go out into the streets and besmirch themselves with vile deeds. Juliette agrees and, on Durand's recommendation, they make their way to the harbour. In response to Juliette's accusation, Durand admits she is intoxicated, but down to the harbour they go anyway. A crowd of sailors and dockers gathers round and Durand promises them that her companion is going to satisfy their every desire. Juliette seats herself on a bollard prepared to co-operate, but soon finds herself carried aloft on the penises of two sailors, penetrating bow and stern. "Wait," says Durand, "give her something to hold onto," and puts a large penis in either hand. She then presents her hindquarters to another sailor. Juliette alone satisfies fifty men, and then afterwards they dine with them in disgusting conditions; Durand genially distributes free doses of poison to anyone who wants somebody done away with...'*

He put the book down on the table. 'Are you glad that you have done that?' he said to X. 'Maybe not, maybe we should do something different, something a little less unforgiving. What about this? Sex and dying dogs.'

'...The choice is between the operating table and the floor. He spreads out the blanket on the floor, the grey blanket underneath, the pink on top. He switches off the light, leaves the room, checks that the back door is locked, waits...'

'It's a dog's life,' said Freddie, 'if that is all you can do. If you want to smoke why smoke a cigarette, smoke a cigar. Heroes always smoke cigars – cigars that have been rolled on the tight cheeks of a thigh. Rolled while those that roll them listen to a reader read a love story.' Freddie looked at X as he lay on the bed. X looked satisfied. He almost leered.

X lay on the wet sheets. Sweat ran from under his arms. His stomach was covered in his own semen. He closed his eyes. Then he wept.

'The day I left Mozambique, if you knew what I went through,' X murmured. 'If you knew how much I loved you, how much I still love you.' X put out his hand and stroked his face. 'I tried to stay away from this room. I tried to not remember you. I thought I would never see you again. I thought you were out of my life.'

He watched X. He walked over to the window. 'But you did not look back for me from the window of the train,' he said. He watched the revolving light that hung on one of the tall buildings outside the room. It was a revolving advertisement, an advertisement for a new kind of telephone – a new kind of communication. Then he walked over to the mini bar. There was a bottle of sparkling wine inside it. He took out two glasses from the cupboard just above it.

'And a glass for me,' said Freddie. 'Sparkles make me feel good, and I feel like feeling good. And now I know what it is you will do.'

He walked over to where X lay. 'Why did you keep your

marriage a secret?' he asked X.

'I wanted to be with you too much,' X replied. 'And I thought that Y, my wife, was descending into a different world to mine. I thought she was in some ways dead to me, dead to the world that I want and the world that I know. I was frantic. I tried to get friends to intervene, but they could not. And then when I came back here I saw her again. I saw her hair and I saw her face, and I knew that I needed to stay with her so that I could help her. But I had nothing left except the memory of you, and the memory of a dead wife.'

'It is a story that has no ending,' he said to X. 'What about now?'

'Now, I don't know. Now I just need to have the strength to help her get out and to stay with you. Stay with me here. Let Y go in your place. And then we can be together. We can live together in my house, in the green suburbs with a golden dog. You will help her now – help her to get to a place where she will be safe. I can no longer fight for her. I can no longer think.'

'I will think,' he said. He raised his glass. The bubbles floated to the top of the liquid, and then they burst. Each little bubble made a small popping sound as it broke through the surface of the liquid. Then the bubbles were gone.

He raised his glass and looked at X. 'Here's looking at you, kid.' Somehow their positions were now reversed. Somehow the words that they used were the same words. But now Freddie was no longer sure who should say them.

XVII

Freddie packed her suitcase. She wondered why Freddie did this. She was not going anywhere. She still had one night left at the hotel. The newspaper had expected her to be in the city for at least four days, time to go to the conference and time to sit down at a meeting with the editor. Only the meeting with the editor had occurred. The meeting had gone well, she thought as she lay on the bed and yawned. Freddie moved around her, folding jeans and T-shirts.

'We think you should stay in Mozambique for a while. It is expensive for us, but it seems as if your stories of the blood shedding keep our readers happy. And there is talk around town that the drug trade is spreading its wings to Maputo. Nigerians you know. They can easily get in there and it is so easy for them to smuggle drugs in a war. What are our police looking for? Guns, not drugs. So they just march right on through, shooting their way inwards. No, stay there and when you are no longer useful to us we will recall you.' The editor had said nothing about how long they would want her to stay. But she no longer cared because she knew that she would not leave Johannesburg anyway. Johannesburg was where X was.

'Well,' said Freddie to her, 'you actually don't know who will go. I may decide that you remain here with X. You can live happily ever after as they say in the fairy stories. I may decide that you return to Regina and the eyeless room in Maputo. I have not yet made up my mind who will stay and who will get onto the plane. Maybe it will be X. Maybe it will be Y. Maybe it will be you. But there is only one air ticket to this Promised Land. Only one ticket, which will take whoever it is out of this war and place them in another one.' Freddie continued to pack the suitcase.

She wondered what Freddie was putting into it. She had very little clothing with her. Most of it had been left with Marina at the small guesthouse in Maputo. And some clothes were still in the refugee camp. Were they still there, she wondered, or had the doctors used the material as swabs for the dying?

Freddie sat down on the chair opposite the bed. 'If you go, you will go back to writing about the absurdity of the war. How much more can you write I wonder? People love reading about the blood and the legless, but they care fuck all about who is fighting whom. It could be a war anywhere – a war in Palestine or South America. What do they care? They only want to see the blood and if they can't see it on television then the next best thing is to read about it.

'And if X gets onto the plane, what will he do in the Promised Land? He can't stay at a beach resort forever. In any event the last time he was there he was with you so that was the way in which he passed his time. He can't sell cordless telephones in Maputo, and there is not enough electricity surging through the wires for him to set up videoconferences.

'And Y? I suppose it is best to send her on that plane. If the smugglers are marching through the war – drug smugglers, not guns like Rimbaud – she could fit in quite well there. She would have a job; she would be doing something that means something to her. Hmm... Maybe Y. Yellow hair in a dark country. It would look good in the movie, the black and white movie.'

'What will they do with her if the police arrest her here?' she said. 'This isn't the same kind of war – Germany or occupied France or Mozambique. They pretend that they believe in justice. They can't just execute a person. Surely they will just fine her a few, well whatever the currency is here? And there is no proof that she has been involved in any of the murders. But you might as well let her go if X is afraid.' She thought that if she encouraged Freddie to let Y go to Maputo she would get to stay alone with X.

But Freddie did not care. She was going to write the story anyway. 'I wouldn't get too interested in X and Y,' Freddie said. 'If by any chance you were to help her escape, I might have to think more about you and X in the suburbs.'

'What makes you think I would stick my neck out for her?' she said.

'You might just do it because you think that you have a life here with X. It's an excellent reason.'

'But who do you want to put on that plane?' she persisted.

'I don't know. I am still thinking about it. What would go well with the story.' Freddie did not mind what she said. She knew that whatever words she used in this conversation, nothing would change. What would be best? How did they do it in the movie, she mused.

'Let's go,' said Freddie. 'I have finished here. I wonder if there will be the watchdogs at the airport. They are always there watching the African planes leave. Maybe they think people are off to join the African National Congress, but really a plane from Jan Smuts would be the last place that they would leave from. And the drug traders. The watchdogs do not even know what they're looking for. They have a picture of a junkie in their heads. Thin veined, emaciated, haggard. Don't they know by now that the big boys look like Anglo-American employs them? Although I suppose their colour is wrong. But they do wear the Armani suits and hold the phones to their ears just as the plane is closing its doors.'

And so they left Johannesburg. And so they left Rick's Café. And so they left it for whoever would be there after they had gone. And who would be there now, Freddie thought. Or will Rick's Café just disappear like everything else in this book once it is finished? Amil... there will be a black smudge on the pages. The barefoot doctors, I suppose they are still around. Only now they are in Afghanistan. War zones, just different ones.

The air was thick with heat, although Johannesburg did not have the humidity of Maputo. But it had a long drawn out wind that blew the dust into the corners. The rental car moved forward as if by itself, but she knew that Freddie drove it. She closed her eyes and wondered where she was going.

Once again the airport was filled with people, white people. The loud speakers kept announcing the different flights. She listened as an announcer informed the crowded space that the flight bound for Lisbon had been delayed. Something to do with the fact that two of the passengers did not have the right passports.

'Hold your bag carefully,' Freddie said. 'I will carry the suitcase. I don't want your passport to be stolen. That would be too predictable. And then all of you may have to remain behind.'

She scanned the crowd. Where had Freddie said she should meet X and Y?

'Inside the Pizza Hut,' Freddie said. 'They will be at a table eating a pizza with anchovies on it.'

'But why do they need to be eating a specific kind of pizza?' she asked. It is not as if I won't recognise them. Well, at least I will be able to recognise X, if not his wife.'

'Well, that is what they will be eating,' Freddie said. 'They may just eat anchovies for no reason at all.'

'Okay,' she said, 'maybe I can ask for a slice of it when I find them. When do we check in for the flight?' she continued.

'At the last moment,' Freddie answered.

She walked across the milling people, bumping into them as she moved forward. She did not see these people. She just looked for X.

'Don't worry. He will be there,' Freddie said.

She walked into the restaurant. And then she saw them. X took a bite from the pizza. A woman with yellow hair sat opposite him. She was not eating. Freddie sat down at the table next to X and Y. She walked up to X. He saw her and stood up. Then he walked, well, he almost ran towards her. But it was Y whom she looked at. Y, the woman who had walked down the street with her. The woman she had thought, just for a moment, that she could fall in love with.

Well, I can save her now, she thought. I can save her for a

future time when I may want to be in love with someone else.

'Darling, darling,' X spoke softly. 'My wife thinks that I am leaving with her. I haven't yet told her that she's leaving alone.'

'Don't tell her,' she said.

'But it is all right, isn't it?' X continued. 'Everything is still all right?'

Freddie watched the tableau before her and smiled. She now knew what she would do with them. She smiled as she picked up her pen. Her computer lay at her feet but she did not have time to set it up. The idea may be forgotten if she did not write it down just while she thought about it. Y stood up. She walked towards them.

I wonder if X has told Y that he fucked a boy, Freddie wondered. I did not. I wonder if he did.

'I don't know how to thank you,' Y said, her yellow hair caught in the corner of her mouth as she spoke. She wiped it away. Then Y smiled at her. She knew that they had met before. And she knew that she had been interested in something more than just talk. But she knew that she had work to do, so she had put her outside her mind.

'Save it. We still have lots of things to do,' she replied. She wrinkled her nose up as if there was something in the air that she did not care for. But that was a lie.

Y was persistent though. 'Come, sit down. I know a good deal more about you than you suspect. I know for instance that you are in love with a man. It is perhaps strange that we should be in love with the same man.' Y looked over at X. 'The first time I met you, yes, here in the airport, I thought something. Then I met you again and I knew something. I knew there was something between you and X. Since there is nobody to blame, I demand no explanation. I only ask one thing. I think that you will not give me the air ticket; you want to be with X. All right. But I want X to be safe. I ask you as a favour to give the air ticket to X so that you can take him away from me and the squalor and Johannesburg.

'You love him that much,' she said.

'Apparently you think of me only as a drug dealer. Well, I am also a human being. Yes, I love him that much.'

She picked up her glass and held it to her lips. She drank. Freddie could see the yellow liquid swirl in the glass and cling to its sides. A whisky. Alcohol always dims the senses, Freddie thought. That is why most people disapprove of it early in the day. Strange how people believe that senses can only be dimmed as the light fades. What would Y be like if she did not drink? Plain and bookish, I suppose.

'I brought some money for you,' X said to Y. 'Keep it. You may need it in Maputo.' Y smiled at X. It was a smile that said nothing.

The loud speaker made a sudden sound. 'Flight LMA 456... Calling all passengers for Flight LMA 456. Check in will be closed in ten minutes.'

She looked at Freddie. 'Okay,' Freddie said, 'let's go.' Freddie got up from the table and walked towards the check-in counter. She followed Freddie. Then Freddie took the air ticket out of her black bag. X went to the desk where a woman sat next to a till. He paid for the anchovy pizza. Y drained her glass and followed X. And then, in a line, they walked out of the restaurant.

'Y... You are under arrest... on a charge of being an accessory to the murder of a civilian in Berea and dealing in cocaine, mandrax and cannabis,' a voice said out of the bright lights of the concourse. It was the same policeman who had spoken to her in the hotel, in Rick's Café. He was still dressed in his policeman blues. Next to him was a young policeman who looked as if he had not yet started to shave his beard. His face was smooth.

Freddie laughed as she looked up. She continued to walk. X looked at Freddie. 'Give me the ticket,' he said. 'Give it to Y, please...' X's face was white, but it always had been. 'What are you doing?' X pleaded. 'Please...'

'The explanation is quite simple,' Freddie said to him. 'Love, after all, has triumphed over virtue. But it is my love, not yours.'

Freddie turned away from X and Y. 'Come,' she said to her, 'we have to check in for our flight. This suitcase is so very heavy,' she said to a policemen who stood at the barrier. 'Can you help me carry it? It is not very far to the check-in and look, there is no one there any more so we will not have to wait.' The policeman nodded his head and picked up the bags.

'If you don't mind,' said Freddie, 'can I ask you to please help us to fill out the departure forms. With her name.' And Freddie did not point towards Y.

'Why, why are you doing this?' she said to Freddie. She pushed at Freddie. She almost started to shout, but then she realised that it would do no good. 'Why?'

'You are getting on the plane,' said Freddie. 'You. Not either of them. You are getting on that plane.'

Then she knew that she would never see X again. And there was nothing more she could do.

X looked at her. Her intention was clear to him.

'Last night we said a great many things,' she said. 'You said I should do the thinking for both of us. Well, I have done a lot of it since then and it all adds up to one thing. I am getting on that plane to Maputo. I do not belong in this city. You do, with or without Y. Maybe she will go to jail for a short time and then once she gets out you can resume where you left off. You are part of her. You are the thing that keeps her going. If she leaves you here and I stay with you, one day you will regret it. Maybe not today, maybe not tomorrow, but soon, and for the rest of your life.'

'Which you won't have after I have finished this novel,' Freddie interjected.

She continued to speak. Her voice was impassioned. 'We will always have Xai Xai. We didn't have it until I met you again in Johannesburg. We got it back last night. And anyway I have a job to do. Where I am going you can't follow. What I have to do you cannot be any part of. I'm no good at being noble, but it doesn't take much to see that the problems of three little people don't amount to a hill of beans in this crazy world of ours. Someday you will understand that.'

X's eyes filled with tears. But they did not fall.

'Come,' said Freddie, 'we have to go now.'

Quietly she put out her hand and touched X on the cheek. 'Here's looking at you, kid,' she said. X did not know what to say. There was nothing left for him in the script.

Freddie stopped walking and looked at him. Suddenly she felt pity for this man whom before she had found so worthless. She walked over to where X stood. 'She tried everything to make me put your wife on that plane. She even tried to convince me that she did not want to stay just for you, and that Y did not love you anymore. I let her pretend, as I knew what I was going to do anyway.'

X did not look at Freddie. He did not look at Y. He remained fixed to the floor. His eyes stared at her, the imprint of his face reflected off the bright camera lens.

'Welcome to the fight,' Freddie said to X. 'This time I know that our side will win.' Under her breath, Freddie murmured, 'I am not sure which side is which, but what does it matter? When did it ever matter?'

'What you did for X,' she said to Freddie as they walked across the tarmac towards the plane, 'that was a fairy tale to make him feel that it was okay to stay with Y and to keep watch over her no matter what happened. I think he knew you were lying.'

'It might be a good idea for us to disappear for a while,' said Freddie. 'Come, I think we can start a beautiful friendship all over again. And maybe I can write another story with you as the main character in it. What about *The Maltese Falcon*? It has a different tone to it. You could be a private dick.'

As she climbed the stairs that led up to the aeroplane she wondered how much blood had been shed in Mozambique since she had left. Already the obsessive fire that she had in her body was burning out, had burnt out. She did not feel sad. The sadness was a smouldering burnt-out ember, subtle, only warm. She suffered no longer in her heart, and only felt a slight twinge of guilt to think that she did not even suffer in her head.

She turned to look backwards before she entered the aeroplane door. X had already walked away.

XVIII

There were more journalists at the refugee camp that day than had been there ever before, and nothing had changed. Amil still had no legs and the woman with the carved-out scarring on her cheeks only had the company of ghosts in the place of her husband and three children. The woman talked to them daily, sometimes small soft sounds as she murmured to one of her children, sometimes a loud shout as she called her husband. Daily she would follow the road where the land mine had been planted, the road that lead from the village to the river. She followed it alone. She went to collect water for her children.

And Diana, the future Queen of England, had arrived.

The Princess came in a bright red Manificio, the smallest jet to be built, its body surrounded by weapons. It had been especially flown out from Britain in order to take her from Maputo airport to the north. As he heard them, he looked up. A harsh sound, it could have been an animal sound but he knew it was not. It was too foreign, too hard. And then he saw them. Four jet planes flew around the red Manificio. From a tiny snarl in the distance the noise suddenly became a great tearing call. A call to the arching blue sky. The four fighter planes were flying in perfect formation around the centre of red, lustrous like winged angels with cutting noses. They flew perfectly together and then they climbed. They were so relaxed; they seemed to be tied together by a piece of invisible string. Then they reached a point and unwrapped the red craft and moved, each one to different points of the earth. And then they were gone leaving only four trails of silver web. It all happened so quickly.

And they called the Princess brave.

She stepped out of the twelve-seater aircraft wearing a sky blue dress sprinkled with diamonds. It flapped round her knees – those well formed perfect knees – as she walked. It had no sleeves; tiny thin lacy straps fitted themselves over her shoulders. Maybe she should have worn khaki, this princess. Khaki, the colour of the sand, but she did not. She was not a tourist, she knew about fashion. She knew about the photograph, she must be a princess. The air was hot and dry, but the dust did not settle in the dimmed gold of her hair or on that beautiful dress. Dust suspended in the air. Maybe it kept away because she was a princess, or maybe it was those glittering diamonds that chased the particles far from her.

He recognised the dress. He had seen one like it in the *Vogue* magazine that he had bought at the Johannesburg airport when he had left X and Y. He bought *Vogue* magazine to distract himself. Beautiful pictures, pictures of something other than his own hunger. The clothes always looked like exhibitions, photographic exhibitions, draped across those beautiful bodies, the art of bodies. When he bought the magazine and was leafing through the pages as he sat on the aeroplane he had known that he would never see this dress on a living person. Just as he knew that he would never see Y again. But here was the dress. Someone was wearing it, a real live doll. Could it be that he would find Y again? The dress, Donatella Versace had boasted on the pages of *Vogue*, cost over four thousand pounds – one of the most expensive dresses ever made.

And the people in the camp came out to greet this princess and her dress. They crawled out from under the rocks and from inside the tents. It was as if the whole of that small world stood still, stopped breathless, for a vacant princess, as vacant as their vacant world.

Click, click went a thousand cameras, *write, write* went a thousand pens, *tick, tick* went a thousand portable computers. They were the lucky ones whose computers never seemed to need to be charged, their batteries ran on and on, never giving up. The princess in her sky-blue dress picked up children who had no arms. She comforted men and women who had nothing left except the belief that maybe, just maybe, somehow this visit would make a difference. And for now there were the smiles and the laughter and the hope. And the visit did make a difference, but not to them.

What now, wondered Freddie. She turned to him. 'You had better write up this story. I have made you a writer. Describe the dress, *haute couture*. Describe how much the visit costs. If you don't know I am sure you can just make it up. More than enough money to feed, clothe and shelter the people in the camp for at least a year. Remember that I want you to have moral integrity. Make it clever and smart and witty. Write as if you are writing for *Vogue* magazine.'

He looked up at Freddie from where he sat. 'I am tired of all of this now. It all seems so desperate. I want something else,' was all he said.

'Wait,' Freddie replied, 'we are nearly at the end of the story. This will be the last chapter, a grand finale.'

The other journalists who sat around him were excited. They anticipated something. Something out of the ordinary would happen on this day with a fairytale princess who came from a world where we are all the fairies that we want to be.

'I can smell her, even from here,' he said to Freddie, '*And the jessamine faint, and the sweet tuberose, / The sweetest flower for scent that blows.* Shelley – perfume has always been an inspiration to the poets, why not to a journalist?'

'Whatever,' Freddie replied. 'You can write whatever you want to.'

'It is the illusion of romance that I like,' he thought. 'Maybe I can write a romantic story. I wonder if that will be sensational enough for the readers of the paper, sensational enough for the editor behind his electric fence.'

The scent of the princess wove its smell over the red dust and the tents and the people. A mixture of the blossom of the bitter orange tree mixed with rose oil and a little bit of frankincense. The product of years of work. Years of love. Distilling and mixing the creation of a secret. He could imagine how it was made. A little bit of the orange tree added to the rose, a bit too much, too floral, so add the frankincense, making it spicy, more exotic. The rich top notes still there, soon to make way for the heart of the scent. Sensuous. A gift to a king, but here it was to a queen, a future queen. A quixotic smell, sweet like a child's caresses, the erotic movement of the bow over the strings of the violin, rich and corrupt.

The princess moved over to a royal table. A child, who had arms but no face, clung to the hem of her dress leaving a mud-dark mark on the delicate fabric. Then, with hands so soft, the child lovingly caressed the skin of her divine, smooth, immaculate thigh. This child would not touch white flesh again. The child knew he had to savour the pleasure of this caress. The princess leaned down and held the child's hand, white against black, then she forgot about him and took the cup of tea that had been specially brewed for her. The scent of Earl Grey tea, mingled with her perfume – the aroma of a heart.

And the day was a success. The princess of darkness is a gentle woman. She picked up enough children, caressed enough curly dirty heads, looked compassionately enough at legs that were lost. There was ample colour for photographs to make up a whole film. A film of this day, heat and beauty mixed together, a film for posterity.

He looked up as the princess made her way across the dusty tarmac, still beautiful, still clean and still sweetly smelling. '*Crack*.' The sound came from nowhere. It moved through the dark red dust. And then the same sound again, '*Crack*'. In slow motion he saw one of the princess's bodyguard's jump forward ready to give his life for this sweet person. The first bullet caught her in the face. A small red hole appeared where the eye was. Blood dripped onto the front of her blue Versace dress. A piece of jewellery, blood red, made especially for this moment, a ruby set in between diamonds. The hole where the eye had been stared ahead. It was also blood red. A bloody star that shone brightly. The second bullet found the fresh white ripe flesh of her upper arm. It split the bone so the flesh burst outwards. She made no sound as she fell backwards, this princess. Then she sunk slowly downwards into the dark, gracefully. He thought he heard her whisper something like, 'kill the bastards', but he could not be sure if it were she that said these words.

Bright red, red, like the sky at night, red like the ruby the Indian nurse wore in her nose, red, red... Red for the dead child, the child princess, red, red...

A shadow hovered over her face; he could not tell what shadow it was. Maybe it was one of her guards, black against blue, his mouth against hers, his hands pushing down on where her eye had been. He tried to stop the flow of blood. And the jewel shone on, a hard stone hole reflecting the light of the sun. And the dust moved inwards to stake its claim. Where it had never dared to tread in life it trod now, settling in her hair, covering her bare arms, lying on her face. He could no longer smell her perfume. Its heart was no longer there.

Screams rent the air. Someone shouted a command. Round up the usual suspects. People ran everywhere, and those that could not run moved with the runners. They were carried by a wave. Freddie sat next to him at the table. They were the only two who did not move, watching, thinking, wondering what to do with this story.

'But this never really happened,' he said to Freddie.

'No, it didn't,' she replied, 'but what does it matter? It has happened here for you to write about. And it's a horrible event. The world is accustomed to all kinds of absurdity. The loss of a princess, or even a universe, is not really worth taking seriously.'

And as he sat, Freddie forced him to think about the transience of life, the enigmas of life, which so torment us all. He didn't want to say anything but she made him. She made him speak words, which were almost poetic.

'I wonder what her grave will look like,' he said to Freddie. 'The green of the English earth, the trees in the graveyard garden, the flowers growing upward springing life-like from the beds. God must be a bit like a gardener, making life from death.' He didn't really want to say this. He just said it as he had no other option. He continued, 'Mary Magdalene when she first saw Christ rise from the grave thought he was a gardener,' he continued. He thought about a Mary Magdalene, and of that dress, that sky-blue dress from the pages of *Vogue*. Now it was only a photograph, a ruined dress. And Mary Magdalene was also ruined. 'Maybe the prince of darkness is a gentleman,' he rambled on, 'maybe, just maybe the princess is already having a great time.'

And as he sat in the sun and the dust he thought about Y. He wondered what it would be like to touch her cunt and smell her lingering lilac smell of sweat. He thought he may just be in love with Y…

Epilogue

The first words of this story will be, 'Hey Mister, I met a man once when I was a kid'…

END

Acknowledgements

The author acknowledges the direct and indirect use in the text of the words in the play *Everybody Goes to Rick's* by Murray Burnett and Joan Alison; and both the screenplay, by Julius J Epstein, Philip G Epstein and Howard Koch, and the mise-en-scène, of the film *Casablanca*, released in 1942 by Warner Brothers.

'*What is the point of war without love*'
Saul Bellow: *The Adventures of Augie Marsh*. Penguin Classics, 1996

'*Two clichés in a story can make you laugh, a hundred clichés, they will move you... extreme banality allows you to catch a glimpse of the sublime...*'
Umberto Eco: *Travels in Hypereality*. (Translated by William Weaver) Picador, 1987

'*...Despite the fact that Durand is almost fifty, Juliette declares herself well satisfied with the exchanges and denies that she regrets murdering Clairwil. The two women, having reaffirmed how alike they are in mind and passions, indulge in vigorous sexual relations; Juliette confessing that she never had dealings with a woman who so thoroughly commanded the arts of imparting physical pleasure. They drink a good deal and Durand suggests that they go out into the streets and besmirch themselves with vile deeds. Juliette agrees and, on Durand's recommendation, they make their way to the harbour. In response to Juliette's accusation, Durand admits*

she is intoxicated, but down to the harbour they go anyway. A crowd of sailors and dockers gathers round and Durand promises them that her companion is going to satisfy their every desire. Juliette seats herself on a bollard prepared to co-operate, but soon finds herself carried aloft on the penises of two sailors, penetrating bow and stern. "Wait," says Durand, "give her something to hold onto," and puts a large penis in either hand. She then presents her hindquarters to another sailor. Juliette alone satisfies fifty men, and then afterwards they dine with them in disgusting conditions; Durand genially distributes free doses of poison to anyone who wants somebody done away with...'
Marquis de Sade: *Justine and Juliette*. Productions, Liber SA, 1984

'... The choice is between the operating table and the floor. He spreads out the blanket on the floor, the grey blanket underneath, the pink on top. He switches off the light, leaves the room, checks that the back door is locked, waits...'
J M Coetzee: *Disgrace*. Secker & Warburg, 1999

Other fiction titles by Jacana

African Psycho
by Alain Mabanckou

All is Fish
by Kirsten Miller

Beginnings of a Dream
by Zachariah Rapola

Death in the New Republic
by David Dison

Six Fang Marks and a Tetanus Shot
by Richard de Nooy

Ice in the Lungs
by Gerald Kraak